"No," Christie said, hoping she sounded more certain than she felt. "Not now. Not tonight..."

"Why?"

"Because there's too much unresolved between us."

"This might be a good opportunity to resolve some of those issues," Cal said, no longer kissing her skin but still holding her tightly against his hard body and the soft couch.

"I don't think making love will resolve anything. I think it will just make our lives more complicated and confusing."

Cal moaned against her shoulder, "You think too much, Christie."

She pushed and he levered himself away. She scooted off the couch, her shorts and top badly crumpled and her emotions in a jumble. "Someone has to think for both of us," she said as she flipped her hair out of her eyes. "I'm going to bed—alone."

Dear Reader,

I've learned, in the past thirty-four years I've lived here, that Texas is a state rich in honor and tradition, especially among the original settlers and ranching families. Sometimes, such devotion to principle might even be seen as stubbornness.

The men of the Crawford family of Brody's Crossing are single-minded in their convictions. When I wrote Troy Crawford's story, *Temporarily Texan,* I knew I had to write his older brother Cal's story, as well. Cal's family traditions and his personal history shaped him more than most heroes I've "met" in the more than twenty books I've written. Of course, Cal deserves (and gets!) a very independent, smart and caring woman in Christina Simmons. He thought she was special when they spent two days—and nights—together in Fort Worth before his military service in Afghanistan, but knew she could be only a weekend fling. That was before he returned to find the consequences of their actions.

I hope you enjoy Christie and Cal's story. And if you think these are the last of the Crawfords, don't be surprised if the brothers discover one more family secret in the upcoming months. I would love to hear from you via my Web site, www.victoriachancellor.com. Have a wonderful summer filled with your own discoveries, and I hope you'll look for more BRODY'S CROSSING stories beginning in December, when the town's mayor, Toni Casale, is reunited with her former love, the dashing and successful Wyatt McCall.

Victoria Chancellor

An Honorable Texan
VICTORIA CHANCELLOR

HARLEQUIN®

TORONTO • NEW YORK • LONDON
AMSTERDAM • PARIS • SYDNEY • HAMBURG
STOCKHOLM • ATHENS • TOKYO • MILAN • MADRID
PRAGUE • WARSAW • BUDAPEST • AUCKLAND

ISBN-13: 978-0-373-75219-5
ISBN-10:   0-373-75219-5

AN HONORABLE TEXAN

ABOUT THE AUTHOR

Victoria Chancellor married a visiting Texan in her home state of Kentucky thirty-five years ago, and has lived in the Lone Star State for thirty-two years after a brief stay in Colorado. Her household includes her husband, four cats, a very spoiled miniature pinscher, an atrium full of tortoises, turtles and toads, and lots of visiting wild critters. Last year she was blessed with both a new son-in-law and a granddaughter. Her former careers include fine jewelry sales, military security and financial systems analysis. She would love to hear from you via her Web site, www.victoriachancellor.com, or P.O. Box 852125, Richardson, TX 75085-2125.

Books by Victoria Chancellor

HARLEQUIN AMERICAN ROMANCE

To my editor, Kathleen Scheibling,
for making my books better, and for her patience
with my sometimes humorous and
embarrassing errors of omission.

Acknowledgments

Thanks to SSG Kenneth Marion, U.S. Army, Plano,
Texas, for his help with the army reserves and active
duty details. Any errors or literary license are mine.

Also, thanks to Beverly Brown
of the Lucky B Ranch in College Station, Texas,
for her help understanding and appreciating bison,
and for all bison ranchers and organizations who
have useful information on their Web sites.

Chapter One

Christie Simmons put her Cadillac SRX into Park but didn't turn off the engine. She didn't plan to get out of the car unless a certain tall, tan, brown-haired rancher exited the ranch house and asked what the heck she was doing on his property.

She waited, but no one came out. Which meant he probably wasn't home yet.

But he was coming home, any day now. That's what his brother's fiancée had told her on the phone yesterday. That's what the nice waitress at the café in town had told her. Christie knew small towns had very active grapevines. By now, they'd probably be buzzing with news that a blond "city girl" had been asking about Cal Crawford.

A blond city girl with a nine-month-old baby, Christie corrected herself, turning to look at the rear-facing car seat. She could only see his cute little face in the special infant mirror attached to the backseat. Peter slept as he usually did when she drove long distances—just like a baby. If she stayed parked here too long, though, he'd awaken and want a bottle, some attention or his diaper changed. Maybe all three. She'd rather find a place to stay before Peter started fussing. A bed-and-breakfast, or even a motel would do, as long as it was clean and safe.

Still, she sat for a minute longer, returning her attention to the beige brick ranch house with the green trim. It was neat and well maintained, as was the red barn maybe half a football field away. In the pasture surrounding the yard, black-and-white cows—the kind in those cheese commercials—grazed on newly greening grass. In another pasture, bison, of all things, appeared to be dozing in the noontime sun. On a rocky hill, chickens of every color pecked among the stunted shrubs and clumps of cactus. What a strange and wonderful place!

Especially for a city girl, she thought. She was rarely around animals, except for her mother's overindulged, yappy and slightly asthmatic Pekingese, Mr. Boodles. Christie had always wanted a yellow Lab, but her parents had insisted big dogs were too much trouble, so she'd lavished her attention on her friends' pets.

When Peter was old enough, she'd get him that yellow Lab she'd never had as a child. She'd have a yard for him to play in and one of those cute inflatable kiddie pools. When Peter and the dog got wet and dirty, she'd clean them up and laugh with them, not scold them for making a mess.

She would not raise her child as she'd been raised, in a luxurious but cold home where perfection was more important than happiness.

With a sigh, she circled back onto the drive leading to the county road. She passed under a wooden arch that spelled out Rocking C in rustic iron letters. She was sure Cal had told her that four generations of Crawfords had lived on the ranch. She also had a vague memory of him mentioning he raised Hereford cattle. She recalled those red-and-white animals from the annual Fort Worth Fat Stock Show. She'd dutifully attended for years as the child of one of the rodeo sponsors. Everyone who was anyone in Fort Worth had ties to the Fat Stock Show, the Bass Performance Hall or the Kimball Art Museum. Maybe all three.

Cal had been gone a year and a half. Perhaps the ranch had changed since he'd been away. Perhaps it wasn't even his any longer.... But, no, his brother's fiancée had mentioned Cal was really looking forward to returning to the Rocking C.

"Soon," she whispered to her sleeping son. "Soon you'll meet your daddy."

She headed into Brody's Crossing to find a place to stay until Calvin Peter Crawford IV came home from Afghanistan.

THE RIDE FROM DFW AIRPORT was damn near as uncomfortable as having four pieces of shrapnel cut out of his face. Granted, three of them had been tiny, but the fourth one had left an ugly gash near his right temple.

He'd been called up for active duty just a few months before his military commitment was due to end. His service had been extended by a year of active duty, and while he was gone, his little brother had completely changed the ranch into some kind of organic, bizarre collection of everything he didn't want: buffalo, dairy cows and free-range chickens. What self-respecting rancher raised those animals when he could have good old regular beef cattle grazing on his acres?

He should never have given Troy the power of attorney that James Brody, their lawyer, had said they needed. That simple document had allowed his brother to do whatever he wanted with the Rocking C while Cal was away. And, dammit, he had. He and Cal had exchanged sometimes heated e-mails over the changes to the ranch and had talked a few times by phone, until Cal had become too frustrated to speak to Troy. Cal figured they didn't have anything else to discuss until he actually saw the ranch.

"You need to stop anywhere along the way?" Troy asked.

"No. If I need anything, I'll go into town later." First, he wanted to get out of the desert fatigues and army-issue boots of Sergeant Calvin P. Crawford IV and into the comfortable, worn jeans, Western shirt and cowboy boots of Cal Crawford, rancher. Then, he looked forward to visiting Dewey's Saloon and Steakhouse, seeing his neighbors and having a few beers with a nice, juicy T-bone. No more MREs or institutional trays of food that made school lunches seem appealing.

"Raven has something planned, just so you know," Troy said as they turned onto Highway 16 and headed north, avoiding the main street and its two stoplights.

"Great." There went his plans for the evening. Troy had mentioned that his fiancée was an organic farmer and weaver from New Hampshire. Cal knew she'd come to Texas due to a mix-up with a garden association and had stayed to "help" Troy make all those changes he'd decided were necessary. Cal had seen a picture of Raven in one of Troy's e-mails—she looked like what their father would call a "hippie." She'd probably serve some kind of vegetarian smorgasbord. Or did folks from New Hampshire have smorgasbords? Maybe not. Cal had lived all his life in Brody's Crossing, Texas, except for basic training, two weeks' service every summer and the deployment to Afghanistan. With any luck, he'd never leave here again.

"Who's invited?"

"Just a few friends and some of our new business associates."

"Don't even get me started on the changes to the ranch."

Troy sighed. "Look, Cal, why don't you just admit that something had to be done? The ranch was failing. You were way too far into the bank for operational loans. You could never have recovered the cost of those Herefords from the market price. I know you liked to look out and see them grazing in the pasture, just like they'd always been there, but—"

"Butt out, that's what. You did what you did. I'm going to do what I have to do."

"You're as stubborn as our old man."

"I think the word is *loyal,* not stubborn. Some of us value the past." Cal didn't understand why Troy was so dead set against the traditions of the Rocking C. Yeah, his life hadn't been perfect, but whose had? Troy had been more of a mama's boy, and when their mother had left the family when he was fourteen, he'd been hurt. Cal knew his brother also resented the fact that he'd been the younger son. Their dad had obviously groomed Cal to run the ranch, and that might chafe Troy a bit, but such was life. The oldest son usually took over the family's responsibilities.

Someday, when he had a son, Cal vowed that he'd groom him the same way. He'd need to be tough to run a ranch.

Of course, first Cal needed to get the Rocking C back to the way it was.

"Just don't take your bad mood out on Raven. All the changes were mine, understood? Just because I chose not to be a rancher doesn't mean I'm ignorant of the cattle industry. I was marketing a new cattle breed, you know."

"Yeah, I know that and I hear you loud and clear. I know just who to blame."

"Hell, Cal, I know you've had a rough time, but your attitude sucks. I'm sorry about Dad's accident. I'm sorry I got to go away to college while you stayed to run the ranch. I'm sorry for the timing of your military service. But I'm glad I could take a leave from my job after my vacation ran out, and I'm glad I got a chance to help the ranch survive. If I hadn't done something, including investing a stack of my own cash into the Rocking C, then you'd be coming back to a foreclosure, no stock and no place to live."

"So you say. I see it differently. And don't talk about my bad attitude when I've been serving my country."

"Oh, please. As if you're more patriotic than the rest of us.

You only joined the reserves because Dad and Granddad and the rest of the men in our family served in the army."

"You're so full of it."

"And you're not? I'm your brother. I think I know you pretty well."

Cal snorted. His brother didn't know him at all. He turned his head and looked out the window as they passed under the Rocking C sign. Troy must have repaired it and painted it black. Just the first of many changes. Fresh gravel crunched beneath Troy's fancy SUV's tires as they drove past repaired fences. Cal didn't want to look into the pastures, where Herefords used to graze.

He had a sick feeling in his stomach, along with a racing heartbeat and overreaching sense of dread. He was finally home, but whose home? Not the one he remembered, that was for sure.

His little brother had taken over his life.

Troy thought he knew so much about running a ranch, about life in Brody's Crossing, about family heritage, but he didn't know everything. He didn't know Cal's secret.

And he never would. No one would.

RAVEN HAD INVITED CHRISTIE to the casual family "welcome home" party for Cal, but she'd declined. For one thing, she had no one to watch Peter. For another, she didn't think springing "Hi, welcome home, you're a daddy" would be the right approach in the midst of a family get-together.

So she'd wait. She'd already waited a year and a half since she'd discovered, to her great surprise, that she was pregnant.

During her marriage, while they'd lived in Europe, she'd been told she couldn't get pregnant. The Italian doctor had been so wrong, she thought, as Peter pulled himself up on the ottoman.

They were staying about ten miles away in Graham since Brody's Crossing had no hotel, motel or bed-and-breakfast.

"All that's about to change," Christie told her grinning son. "Yes, it is." She smiled back at him and stroked his soft, downy hair. Light brown, like his father's. But he had blue-green eyes, like hers.

"We're going to open a motel, aren't we?" she asked as he held on and wobbled, trying to stay upright on the carpet. The idea of running her own business still astounded her, and yet felt so right.

She'd bought the Sweet Dreams Motel in Brody's Crossing just yesterday, paying with a cashier's check from her bank in Fort Worth. The place was a run-down mess, with broken windows, horrid bathrooms and a parking lot so patched it looked like a crazy quilt. The stucco and concrete block walls were cracked in places, and the roof had to be replaced before the next big rain. During the walk-through with the Realtor, they'd disturbed a surly opossum and a family of mice living in the maintenance shed. Birds had flown out of gaps in the siding over the office.

Other than that, it was perfect.

"It will be great," she told Peter, and she believed it. Because despite the neglected motel's problems, it had one thing going for it: retro appeal. The old sign alone had made her want to own the darn thing. A crescent moon and sleeping baby, the name and vacancy sign all outlined in—currently inoperable—neon lights. The style was pure late fifties/early sixties, with a low roof and colored, painted doors and metal railings with geometric shapes. The motel had never been remodeled before it closed in the 1980s, so it was still authentic.

Christie wasn't a remodeler or a decorator, but she knew what she liked. And she absolutely loved the decrepit Sweet Dreams Motel.

She'd already hired a contractor. Brody's Crossing mayor Toni Casale was the best, Christie had been told by several people, and she'd hit it off with the other woman, who was near her age and also a blonde. As a matter of fact, they'd shared a laugh at the fact that two blondes were doing what no men had attempted—opening the old motel, which, according to Toni, was sorely needed in a town with no rooms to rent.

She glanced at the clock. "Aren't you getting tired?" she asked Peter, who had grown bored with standing and had crawled over to his favorite toy, a plastic piano that played the most irritating electronic tunes when he hit the big, primary-color keys. To answer her question, he grinned and began pounding.

Christie hoped they didn't have any close neighbors tonight who objected to her baby's piano music.

She was going to call Cal at the ranch later and arrange a meeting. There was no sense in putting off the news any longer. Perhaps they could have lunch in a public place, like that steakhouse she'd gone to with Toni. Or the cute little café in town, although that would be much more public and people might be able to hear their conversation.

That was her big fear—that Cal would find out about Peter from someone else. That's why she'd been very careful to mention she was a widow, and not to act too interested in Cal when she'd talked to others. She'd developed a friendly relationship with Troy's fiancée, Raven, although she'd never told the other woman about Peter. They'd only talked on the phone. She'd tried to be very careful and respectful of Cal's privacy, just as she would have wanted had she been in the same situation.

Not that she'd ever expected to be a single parent. Or to have her own biological child.

Peter quit banging on the piano and rubbed his eyes.

"Time for your bottle? Ba-ba?" she asked, pushing up from the chair and scooping him off the floor. With Peter on her hip, she went to the little kitchen area of the motel room. As soon as he saw the bottle of powdered formula, he waved his arms and started saying, "Ba-ba-ba." That was his word for bottle. He also said, "Ma-ma-ma," but Christie wasn't sure if that was a true *mama* word or just sounds.

Maybe someday soon he'd learn to say "da-da."

She fed Peter, changed his diaper, then sang to him a little until his eyes closed. Within minutes he was sound asleep in his portable crib.

And Christie had no more excuses to keep her from calling Cal.

AFTER A QUESTIONABLE DINNER of some family favorites and some new-age greenery, all Cal wanted to do was retreat to his bedroom, lie on his familiar mattress and watch a little sports. Mavericks, Rangers, Stars—whatever was in season was fine with him. He probably wouldn't have gone to Dewey's even without the planned dinner and company. He'd spent thirty-five years nearly alone, and the past eighteen months surrounded by troops twenty-four hours a day. He just needed some time to himself.

Tonight, several of his neighbors—along with the guy leasing the pasture for his free-range chickens, a nuisance if Cal ever heard one, and Brian Wilkerson, the man who leased the pasture and the new barn for organic dairy cows—had come to share coffee and dessert. Brian came to the ranch twice daily to feed and milk the cows. The only animals the Rocking C owned were the few Herefords Troy had saved from the original herd, a handful of laying hens, horses and a pasture of overgrown, scraggly bison. The ranch hardly looked the same as when they'd raised nothing but regular beef cattle.

Besides Troy's fiancée, Cal had met another new town resident, his lawyer's bride, Scarlett. She was cute in a quirky kind of way, but definitely not his style. She wouldn't make a good ranch wife. James seemed crazy about her, though.

He nudged off his boots, kicked them in the direction of the closet and settled back on the bed. His bedspread was one of those thin cotton ones with ridged lines, brown just like the trim on the house used to be. He'd missed that damned bedspread. At least Troy and Raven hadn't thrown it out, even though it was a little threadbare in spots.

He'd barely gotten into the bottom of the first inning of the Rangers game when Raven knocked on the door. "You have a call," she said through the closed door.

He swung his legs off the bed and opened the door. "I hope this isn't a solicitation. I don't want a credit card or a cell phone."

"No, it's not one of those. I think you might want to take this call."

"Yeah?" He took the phone from Troy's fiancée, who looked as though she knew something he didn't. "Thanks."

"No problem," she said, and shut the door.

He settled back on his bed. "Hello," he said, wondering who would call him his first night back. Probably one of his friends from the feed store who hadn't come for coffee.

He thought perhaps the caller had hung up, but then a woman's voice said, "Cal?"

"Uh, Christie?"

"Yes! I'm so glad you remembered."

"How could I forget?" How, indeed. She'd been every man's dream of a great weekend. Tall, blond, built, fun, smart and sexy. Very sexy. They'd met at the Barnes & Noble in Fort Worth's Sundance Square on the Friday afternoon before his unit was scheduled to deploy. They'd both carried the same recently released biography and had ordered coffee at the attached café. He'd told her the truth—that he was a rancher who was in the reserves, called up for active duty and set to leave the next week. As far as he knew, she'd told him the truth—she was a widow who lived in Fort Worth and worked in marketing.

They'd spent one fantastic weekend together. He'd never expected to hear from her again, not that he minded she'd called him tonight.

Unless she was some kind of weird stalker…

"What's up, Christie?"

"I'd like to see you, Cal. Maybe tomorrow for lunch?"

"In Fort Worth? I just got home and—"

"No, I'm nearby, in Graham. I could meet you at Dewey's, or, if you'd rather, we could meet in Graham. There are several restaurants here."

"Yeah, I know, but… I don't want to be rude, but what are you doing here?" She seemed to know her way around already.

"I…I just need to see you. I have something to tell you."

"Tell me now."

"I can't. I need to see you."

"I'm not real fond of surprises, Christie."

"Yes, I can imagine you're not, but this is one of those times when you'll just have to trust me."

"Or not."

She didn't say anything for a moment, and he kind of regretted cutting her off at the knees. In a low voice, she said, "Please, Cal."

He paused for a moment, then asked, "You're not dying or anything, are you?"

"No! I'm fine."

"No illnesses that you want to tell me about?" He knew he didn't have anything, since he'd had about a dozen physicals since their weekend together.

"Absolutely not."

Well, hell. His curiosity was piqued. "All right," he said. "Noon at Dewey's."

"We… I'll be there."

"We what?"

"Nothing. *We* just need to talk. I'll see you at noon. Good night, Cal."

"Good night."

He ended the call and sat there on the edge of his bed, wondering what the hell was up. What couldn't she tell him over the phone? Or had that been just a ploy to get him to meet her? She didn't have to resort to games. He would have been glad to see her for a replay of their time together. She'd had some tough luck in her life, though. Her husband had been killed in an accident, and she couldn't have kids. That would be hard for any woman to handle, but she'd shown an inner strength when she'd told him a little about her past.

She'd been one special woman.

Maybe she still was. Maybe he was worrying too much, but he'd learned to be cautious. He'd trusted his brother to take care of the family ranch, and Troy had changed everything. He'd trusted the military to let him out when his time was up, and they'd extended his duty.

What else could possibly happen?

CHRISTIE ARRIVED EARLY, requested a booth near the back and tried not to show Peter how nervous she felt. She settled him in the wooden high chair and spread a handful of finger food on the table in front of him. Oblivious to her worries, he babbled and grabbed a handful.

She would have preferred finding a babysitter for Peter, but she knew so few people: Toni Casale on a professional basis, Raven York via the telephone, the daytime front-desk clerk at the motel in Graham. She didn't know any of those women well enough to ask them to watch Peter while she went to lunch with Cal. Besides, they might not be good with children.

Maybe she should go ahead and hire a nanny. She rarely felt she needed one, but with the upcoming renovations on the motel, perhaps it would be wise to have a professional available to watch the baby. He was crawling and nearly walking, and getting into everything. She had to settle down, perhaps even find a house in Brody's Crossing for a few months until the owner's suite at the motel could be finished.

Unless, of course, Cal absolutely pitched a fit, rudely and publicly denounced her and his son and told her to get out of town.

Would she listen? Her first instinct was no, she would fight. But for what? If he was insistent that he didn't want to acknowledge Peter, maybe they would be better off without him in her son's life. She didn't have to stay in Brody's Crossing. Her nice condo in downtown Fort Worth waited for her, if she chose to move back, or she could buy a house in the suburbs. She wanted to give Cal a chance for all their sakes, but only if he wanted to be a positive part of Peter's life. A bad father was worse than no father at all, in her opinion.

Her own father hadn't been bad, but he hadn't been nurturing and kind, that was for sure. When she'd done something he approved of, however, he'd been generous with his attention and his money. His love, as he defined the emotion, had been conditional.

Oh, why was she worrying so much? Cal would be here soon, and she would know almost immediately how he'd react to the news that they'd created a son together.

"Ba-ba-ba," Peter demanded, banging on the table, scattering finger foods.

"Are you ready for your bottle already?" she asked. "Okay, Mommy's hurrying," she said, digging in the diaper bag on the seat beside her. Once she found it, she motioned the waitress over. "Could I get some warm water, please?"

"Of course. What can I get you to drink?"

"Iced tea would be fine," Christie replied, fishing for the terry-cloth bib she kept for Peter's feedings. "Here it is," she said to the baby, and held it up for him to see.

And sat frozen in place. Standing behind Peter's high chair was the man she'd known for only three days. He wore a plaid Western shirt, jeans and a stern expression on his handsome face. He stood tall and seemed lean, yet more imposing, his shoulders broader. He should have been a stranger, but he seemed so familiar.

That's because you look at a baby version of his face every day.

"Cal," she whispered.

"Christie," he replied, his face tight. An angry red scar cut across his temple, between his eye and his hairline. "What's going on?"

"Lunch," she said, motioning to the other side of the booth.

He sat down, stiff and distrustful, and eyed Peter as if he'd never seen a baby before.

"Cal, this is Peter," she said, and the baby turned his head toward her and grinned when he heard his name. "He's—"

"Here's your hot water," the waitress said, "and your tea." She set both on the table. "Oh, hi, Cal. Welcome home. What can I get for you?"

He looked as if he were trying to force a smile for the waitress, but the gesture came out more of a grimace. He must really be upset.

"Iced tea, please, Twila," he said, then added as soon as the girl left, "and maybe I should have a beer or a shot. What do you think, Christie? Do I need a drink?"

"I don't know, Cal," she replied, getting a bit irritated. "I suppose that depends on how well you take the news that you're a father."

Chapter Two

Christie hadn't meant to blurt it out like that, but he'd acted so…sarcastic. Sure, this was a surprise, but he didn't have to imply he needed to be drunk before finding out he was a father.

Now he was slightly pale, making the scar on his temple stand out even more. He stared at Peter, and the baby stared back, so she took the opportunity to mix the powdered formula with the warm water the waitress brought for his bottle.

Finally, she got the temperature of the formula right and glanced up. Cal was now staring at her. "You aren't breast-feeding."

"No, I couldn't. I tried, but it doesn't always work out."

He looked at her as if it were her fault her milk hadn't come in. Fine. What did he know about babies, anyway? He might know a lot about calves, but Peter didn't have four legs, and she didn't have an udder, and Cal wasn't going to make her feel as if she were less of a mother because she couldn't nurse her son.

"You're sure he's mine?" Cal asked.

"Oh, that's a typical male question," she said, popping the nipple into Peter's mouth. "Of course I'm sure he's yours. We can have a paternity test at any time, although I think that by looking, you can see who he resembles."

"What happened to 'I can't have children'?"

"Obviously, the doctor I saw in Europe was wrong. Or maybe he told me I couldn't have children because of my husband. I don't know! His English was terrible and I don't speak Italian. At the time, all I knew was that I would never be a mother."

"Not the case," he mumbled.

"No, and despite your obvious opinion of the situation, I'm thrilled to have Peter."

"Would that be Calvin Peter Crawford V?"

"No, that would be Peter Simmons Crawford. I took the liberty of giving him your last name and listing you as the father on the birth certificate, although if you don't want to be a part of his life, his last name can always be changed. He's too young to know the difference, and quite frankly, I don't need child support and Peter doesn't need the influence of a reluctant father."

Cal stared intently at the baby as Peter took his bottle, sitting up in the high chair as he now preferred. Gone were the days when he automatically snuggled into her arms and let her feed him. Now he was all about independence. In a few more months, she suspected he'd begin saying, "No, I'll do it myself!"

"*He* might not know the difference, but I do. I'll know. I'll know I missed seeing the first months of my son's life. Missed naming him after my father and grandfathers. So he's what, nine months old?"

"Nine months last Wednesday." She took a deep breath. "And even if you'd known about him, you still would have been away. They don't give a leave because you discover you're going to be a father." She knew because she'd checked.

"No, but I could have seen his pictures. I could have done…something."

"I took tons of photos. I have them all for you, including the ultrasounds."

"Why didn't you tell me, Christie? Write me a letter, an e-mail, or call the ranch?"

"I did call the ranch, but I wasn't about to tell your brother or Raven before I told you. Frankly, I didn't think it was any of their business. I wanted to tell you in person. I didn't think this was something you should find out in a letter or e-mail when you were thousands of miles away."

Cal sat there even after the waitress brought his iced tea and Christie told her they'd order in a few minutes. He sat and watched Peter struggle to hold his bottle, then hurl it across the table when he didn't get it tilted at the right angle to get the formula out. Christie handed the bottle back to her son, and soon he found the right angle and began to suck greedily.

When Peter was just about finished, he hurled the bottle in Cal's direction again. Cal caught it, and when he looked back at Peter, the baby was grinning. He banged his little fists on the table and looked so adorable that Cal smiled back. They stared at each other, and Christie's heart skipped a beat.

She wished she had her camera. She wished she'd thought to document father meeting child.

"I have a son," Cal said softly.

"Yes, you do."

And to complete the moment, Peter squealed and threw a Cheerio at Cal.

"HAVE YOU BEEN TO THE RANCH?" Cal asked after they'd ordered lunch.

"I drove out there, but you didn't appear to be home yet, so I didn't go to the door. The animals are wonderful, though."

Cal snorted. She was such a city girl, thinking animals were "wonderful." She probably didn't know a dairy cow from beef on the hoof.

"Where are you staying?"

"In Graham, for now, but I'll be moving to Brody's Crossing."

"Why? Don't you live and work in Fort Worth?"

"I quit my job a few months before Peter was born, and, yes, I still have my place in Fort Worth."

"So you mentioned you don't need my child support. This might sound a little rude, but how are you getting by?"

She sighed and wiped a little milk from the baby's mouth. *His* baby. Peter.

This was going to take some getting used to.

"I already told you I'm a widow. My husband left me rather well off. And also, I should let you know, I come from a wealthy family. I was working for my father's company, SHG, when we met in Fort Worth. That's Simmons Hotel Group. He inherited a few hotels and expanded the business. I inherited a trust fund."

"Oh." She *was* wealthy. Even he, a small-town rancher, had read about those hotels in the business sections of the paper. Christie Simmons probably had more money than he'd ever see in a lifetime. "So now you're just hanging out in Brody's Crossing and Graham, waiting to see what my reaction would be to the news?"

"Of course I wanted to see your reaction, but I decided to stay in town *before* you came home. Actually, I've bought some property of my own, and I'm starting my own business."

"Yeah?" He was just about to ask what she'd possibly do in Brody's Crossing when Twila brought their food. He'd ordered chicken-fried steak—something he hadn't had in a year and a half—while Christie had chosen a chicken tenders salad. At least she'd found something on the menu she liked. She was obviously more accustomed to eating gourmet food in fancy restaurants.

Not that either one of them had paid much attention to food that weekend they'd spent together.… He shook off the errant thoughts and asked, "What business?"

She shifted and fiddled with her salad before looking back up. "The Sweet Dreams Motel near downtown."

He almost jumped out of the seat. "That old place? It was falling down twenty years ago!"

"I don't doubt that, but it has a certain appeal," she said as she sprinkled a few more little cereal circles on the high-chair tray for Peter.

"That place should have been bulldozed years ago, and would have been, if the city could make it go away."

"No! It's wonderful—it's so retro."

"It's old, that's what it is," he said, stabbing his chicken-fried steak with his fork. "You won't be able to open it as a motel for at least six months. Maybe a year, if ever."

"I'm hoping for a fall opening. Perhaps around Labor Day if I'm lucky." She righted Peter after he leaned sideways in the chair and dropped cereal on the floor.

"That's pretty aggressive. Who's doing the work?"

"Toni Casale's company—Casale Remodeling," she answered before taking a bite of salad.

"She's good, but I'm not sure even she can save that old motel."

"*We'll* save it together. I'm committed to making it into a viable business again. Retro is in. I can get great press from the Dallas–Fort Worth area. It's not too far for a quick weekend trip, which adds to the appeal."

"Well, you're the marketing expert. I just think it's a waste of time." He tried to concentrate on his food, which tasted a lot better than he remembered. Christie planned to open a business here in Brody's Crossing, but she'd also kept her place in Fort Worth. He wasn't stupid; she wasn't really making a commitment to live here. She'd get bored or frustrated with her project and leave. It wasn't as if she needed the money.

"I can understand your reservations about the property,

since you've seen it as only a run-down motel." She shrugged, then flipped her head to send her long blond hair behind her shoulder. "I disagree, of course, but I understand."

Nice of you, he felt like saying, but didn't. He didn't want to argue with her. He didn't care about the old motel. He cared about the fact he now had a son who wasn't named after him, and a former lover who'd *sort of* moved to his hometown while he was recovering from a roadside bomb.

"You can't stay in Graham in a motel for six months," he said after finishing his meal. "That would get darned uncomfortable for anyone, much less with a baby, I imagine."

"I know," she said with a sigh, pushing lettuce around the bowl. "I'm going to look into renting a house here until the owner's suite I'm planning is finished. We're doing that one first, of course, so Peter and I will be able to move in."

He would no doubt regret what he was about to say—if not today, then soon and probably often. But, dammit, he could see that Christie was serious about renovating that old motel, at least for now, and that meant she was going to be in town for months. With his baby. He pushed his plate back and folded his arms on the table.

"Look, now that I'm home, Troy and Raven are leaving tomorrow for New Hampshire. She needs to get back to her farm, and Troy is starting a new job." He paused and drew in a deep breath. "Since you need a place to stay and I've got plenty of room at the ranch, why don't you move in out there?"

"Move in with you?" She sounded slightly appalled.

"Well, yeah. It's not like I'm asking you to do anything but live at the ranch. Frankly, I doubt you'll be able to find anywhere to rent that would be suitable for a baby. My house might not be plush, but it's comfortable and clean. Raven fixed it up a little. Painted the walls and stuff like that."

Christie pushed away her salad bowl. "I'm sure the house

is fine, but…well, we hardly know each other. Won't your friends and neighbors jump to conclusions?"

He shrugged. "I suppose they will. After all, we have a child together."

"You're going to tell everyone that Peter is your son?"

"Of course!" What, did she think he was ashamed of having a son? He wasn't, but she should have named the baby after him, in the tradition of the Crawford firstborn sons. Maybe it wasn't too late to change the baby's name….

"I didn't tell anyone. I wasn't sure how you'd react to the news, so I tried to be careful."

"I've found it's better to be up-front about things my friends and neighbors are going to discover anyway. They can be nosy and sometimes they'll interfere. That's just the way things are in a small town."

Twila came and cleared away their dishes after chatting a bit. Peter began to fuss, then cry. Christie efficiently unlatched the seat belt on the high chair while Cal watched, feeling completely out of his element. He knew nothing about babies. He could shove a bottle in an orphaned calf's mouth, dose him with antibiotics, vaccinate him and do a half dozen other procedures, but he'd never been around a baby. Maybe if he'd had a chance to get used to the baby when Peter was a newborn, he'd feel more confident, but right now, the baby's needs were a complete mystery.

All the more reason to spend time with his son, no matter how scary the idea.

"I think we'll go. I've got to stop by Toni's office, then Peter needs a nap. Besides, I need to consider your offer."

He stood up. "For how long?"

She looked up at him, looking a little frazzled. By the crying baby or by him? "I…I'm not sure. Maybe until tomorrow."

"I'll help you to your car."

"You don't have to," she answered, but he was already picking up the diaper bag. That and the baby carrier were a lot for one woman to carry.

She preceded him out of the Dewey's, Peter held high on her left side, facing backward. The baby watched him as he followed. Cal resisted the urge to make a silly face at the fussing baby. Would that make the little guy laugh or cry? Cal wished he knew. He wished he felt comfortable enough with his child to find out. Of course, they'd just met.

At the front, Christie paused for him to open the door.

Cal stood there, feeling as if he was being watched. He slowly turned and looked around.

Everyone seated in the restaurant section of Dewey's had focused their attention on him. He felt a blush creep up his neck. Damn, what a ridiculous reaction. "Hey," he said to no one in particular.

"Welcome home, Cal," Police Chief Montoya said from a nearby table.

"Cute baby," fellow rancher Rodney Bell said with a knowing smile.

"Yeah, he is, isn't he?" Cal answered. Then he smiled and added, "He's mine."

PETER WENT TO SLEEP as Christie drove to Toni Casale's office just down Main Street past the grocery store Toni's parents owned. The redbrick and black-trimmed two-story building adjoined others and sat right on the wide sidewalk.

A timeline for the renovations needed to be set now. Toni had said she'd check with the subcontractors for availability of work crews for the aggressive opening Christie wanted.

But in truth, she'd do almost anything to keep from thinking about moving into Cal's house, on his ranch. Just her, her baby and her baby's daddy.

She'd never thought of moving in with Cal. She'd envisioned renting a place, if the initial meeting with him went well, and letting father and son get to know each other. Slowly. Then, if she decided to stay in Brody's Crossing, they could *maybe* make other arrangements. She liked Cal, she was still attracted to him, but she didn't want to rush into a relationship.

Spending the weekend with Cal had been exciting, wonderful and…temporary. A weekend didn't make a lifetime. Even when you thought you'd have a lifetime, sometimes you didn't.

A feeling of panic threatened, as it sometimes did when she thought about being a single mother, and she took several deep breaths as she pulled into a parking space in front of the office. Today she felt very much alone. No one else could give her advice, not really, although there were several friends she could ask back in Fort Worth. But she had to make the decision about Cal herself rather than rely on the advice of other people. After all, it wouldn't be them out there, isolated. Especially at night.

She realized she'd been stopped for too long, her SRX in Park and her son asleep in the back. With a shake of her head, she turned off the engine and opened the door. From the backseat she grabbed the diaper bag and unlatched Peter's car seat. Careful not to slam the door, which would wake him for sure, she looped the car seat handle over her arm and walked toward the office.

A nice-looking man exited at the same time she reached for the door, so he held it open for her and Peter. "Thank you," she said softly.

"You're very welcome," he said with a killer grin. Why couldn't Cal be so easygoing? She didn't remember him being as serious and opinionated as he was now. Maybe the military service had changed him, or perhaps he was really upset about Peter.

"Are you here to see Toni?" the man asked, pulling Christie back into the present. "I'm her big brother."

"Yes, I am here to see her. I'm Christie Simmons. I'd shake hands, but I need both to hold the baby."

"Leo Casale. And I completely understand. I'd offer to help, but I don't know anything about babies."

"Thank you, but I'm fine. It's nice to meet you, Leo. Toni mentioned that you own the hardware store."

He smiled again, showing a dimple in his left cheek. Leo was very attractive, looking more like a Nordic god than an Italian entrepreneur. "Makes it convenient for a sister in the renovation business."

Christie chuckled. "I imagine she's a good customer."

"She drives a hard bargain."

"I'm glad to hear that. I'm renovating the Sweet Dreams Motel."

"Really? Wow, that's great. We need a motel in town."

"That's what I've heard…although not everyone feels the same way," she said, thinking again of Cal's negative reaction.

"Who?"

"Oh, never mind," she said with a smile. "I should get inside."

"Of course. He looks like he's really asleep, so maybe I could carry him without waking him up or dropping him."

"No, that's okay. I'm getting used to carrying a nearly twenty-pound baby, a ten-pound car seat and about the same in the diaper bag. It's like taking a workout with me, wherever I go."

He chuckled as he held the door open. She saw him eye the empty ring finger on her left hand. "Nice meeting you, Christie. I'll be seeing you around town."

"I suppose so." If she wasn't mistaken, Toni's big brother had just flirted with her! She'd never piqued a man's interest while holding her baby. "Nice to meet you, too, Leo."

He grinned again and waved as he took off with a long stride down the street.

Toni was in her office, talking on the phone when Christie

entered. Peter was still sleeping, so she took a moment to look around. The small office was more functional than decorative, and Christie admired the exposed red brick, wide crown moldings and copper-colored pressed-tin ceiling. There were very few indications that this was a woman's business. Christie mostly speculated that Toni had planned it that way, to succeed in a male-dominated business.

"Come on in," Toni said as she hung up the phone.

"I thought I'd drop by and see if we could work out a schedule. I have some decisions to make about living arrangements."

"Yes, I imagine you do, with Peter to consider," Toni said, smiling at the sleeping baby.

"I've thought of renting a house." *As opposed to staying with Cal at the ranch.* Peter went to sleep around seven-thirty every night, leaving lots of "alone time" for two adults who hadn't been able to keep their hands off each other when they'd first met. Now, their situation was more complicated, and adding temptation to the mix probably wasn't a good idea.

Toni frowned. "I'm not sure what's available at the moment. We've had several families move here recently, but no new houses built yet. There might be more choices in Graham, but that's a longer drive."

"I was hoping to find something close. It doesn't need to be luxurious or large, just clean and safe for Peter."

"Your best bet would be to check with a Realtor in Graham, since we don't have an office here in Brody's Crossing. I can recommend someone there, if you'd like."

"Yes, that might be best." Christie didn't think Toni sounded very confident that a listing would be available.

"Okay, as far as a schedule, I have had time to talk to my subs," Toni said, taking out a legal pad from her desk drawer.

Over the next few minutes, they discussed an aggressive timetable, based in part on Christie's ability to pay extra for dedicated work at the site. Toni explained that most contractors worked on several jobs at once, splitting their time based on deadlines, weather and material availability. The crews might work anywhere from Decatur to Graham to Olney, tying them up from one day to one week. Also, Brody's Crossing had a slight boom in growth with the new farmers' market, butcher shop and several smaller offices. Then there were always home renovations and repairs.

Just as they finished, Peter started waking up. Christie unlatched him from his car seat. "He's probably wet. Is there a place to change him here?"

"Sure. You can use the little conference room across the hall."

"I'll be right back." She snagged the diaper bag and baby, and was just about to enter the hallway when the door to the main office opened, bringing in a gust of warm air and a tall, angry-looking Texan.

"We need to talk," he said without pleasantries.

"I thought we did that a little while ago." Christie snuggled Peter closer to calm her suddenly pounding heart. Cal had startled her, but she had a feeling that just being around him was disturbing on several levels.

"I've thought of something I should have said earlier."

"I'd rather wait, Cal. I need to think about your offer." Peter began to fuss, and Christie felt like doing the same.

"This needs to be said," Cal insisted, his expression intent.

He'd had about the same expression on his face when he'd braced himself above her, their bodies hot and naked. She shook off the memory and started walking away. "I need to change the baby, and then Toni and I will finish up. Why don't we schedule something later."

"Let's settle it now."

"Oh, hello, Cal," Toni said from the doorway of her office. "Welcome home. Can I help you with something?"

"No. I need to talk to Christie."

Toni looked very surprised. "Oh. Christie, do you want a little privacy?"

Actually, she didn't want to have this conversation at all. "Cal, I think we should talk later."

He braced his hands on his hips. "I don't even know how to get in touch with you, Christie. How are we going to talk?"

"I'll call you."

"Christie, are you okay?" Toni asked.

"I'm fine. I'm sorry for the intrusion." She'd barged into Cal's life; now he was apparently doing the same in hers.

She turned back to Cal. "I said I'd call you, and I will."

"I'll be in my office if you need me," Toni said. "Cal Crawford, you behave yourself."

Cal completely ignored Toni. He drilled Christie with his blue-gray eyes. "Like you called me eighteen months ago?"

"You don't need to be sarcastic," she said, feeling herself flush with anger…and maybe a little bit of guilt. Should she have called him? Her rationale had seemed so reasonable while she was pregnant, and immediately after Peter's birth. And by then, Cal's return was imminent. Of course, he'd been delayed, then wounded.

"Sorry for my bad attitude, but it's not every day a man finds out he has a son!" he said, stepping closer.

"You're lucky to have Peter," she said in an angry whisper, unwilling to tell the world their private business. "I can't believe how angry you've become from the time we left the restaurant to now."

"I'm not angry. I'm…perturbed."

"That's just another word for angry."

"Okay! I'm disappointed you didn't tell me, and I'm concerned the baby doesn't have my full name, as he should, and I'm *angry* Leo Casale was telling his customers at the hardware store that a beautiful blonde and her baby have come to stay in town!"

"He said I was beautiful? How nice." Christie focused on that word and ignored the rest of Cal's rant as she spread the changing pad on the end of the table. She grabbed a diaper and the baby wipes from the diaper bag.

"He's not right for you, and you should just stay away from men who talk too much!" Cal wasn't trying to be quiet or reasonable.

"Hey, that's my brother you're bad-mouthing," Toni's voice admonished from the other side of her almost-closed door.

"You're jealous!" Christie exclaimed as she stripped the wet diaper off Peter. She quickly wiped his baby parts and efficiently secured the tabs on the new diaper before he squirmed away.

"I'm not jealous of Leo Casale."

She held the baby with one hand on his tummy while she placed the baby wipes in the diaper bag. "Sounds like it to me."

"Well, if I am, it's because he doesn't have a right to talk about you as if you're single and looking."

"I'm definitely single, but you're right—I'm not looking." Looking for a nanny, maybe, but not a man.

"See, this is exactly what I came over here to talk to you about, but we got all sidetracked. You're single, and you're a mother. The mother of my baby. It took me a few minutes to figure this out because I was really surprised at Dewey's. Now I know there's only one thing we can do."

"Oh? I can see a lot of ways this could turn out."

"No. We have to do what's best for the baby, and there's only one solution."

She had a horrible feeling that Cal's "solution" would be even worse than his idea of her moving to the ranch.

"We need to get married. Now. As soon as possible."

Chapter Three

"I will not marry you for the sake of the baby. That's a terrible reason to get married!" Christie picked up Peter from the desk and stuffed the pad into the diaper bag.

"People do it all the time. It's the right thing to do."

She patted Peter on the back and looked up into Cal's eyes. His eyebrows were drawn into a straight line and his expression was determined. He was one single-minded man. "Cal, this may come as a shock, but for me, doing what makes me—and Peter, of course—happy is a huge consideration. Marrying for the wrong reasons is as wrong as—"

"Our weekend fling that included unprotected sex?"

At least he'd had the courtesy, if she could call it that, to keep his voice down so Toni didn't hear that little goodie. "That might have been irresponsible of us, but I don't regret what came out of that weekend for anything. I've never been happier than the moment Peter was born."

"Yeah, I would have liked to be there, too," he said. "But happiness isn't everything. There's a right and a wrong way to approach things, and I—"

"I'm not going to listen to this. We are not getting married for the sake of the baby, and if you keep this up, I will not even consider moving to your ranch."

"Are you threatening me?"

"I'm telling you that I won't be bullied into marriage or making a decision. Back off the cave-man tactics or I'll leave Brody's Crossing so fast I'll make your head spin."

"I have a right to see my son."

She shifted the baby to her other shoulder. "Only when and if a court gives you that right. And believe me, Cal, you don't want to continue with the threats. I have excellent attorneys." She turned and walked away before he noticed how truly angry and upset she was.

Why had she thought telling this man about their child would be easy?

Because you don't really know him, a little voice inside her head answered. *Because the only thing you know about him is that he kissed you like you were the only woman in the world, and you didn't want to know anything about him because he was leaving. You just wanted that weekend. Really wanted it.*

Shaking, she handed Peter to Toni. Without a word, she grabbed a card from her purse and wrote her cell-phone number on it. Cal was still standing inside the conference room, breathing deeply as if he were trying to control his anger.

"Here," she said, handing him the card. "That's my cell phone if you feel the need to call me before I make a decision. I'm not trying to threaten you, Cal, but I won't be bullied. I don't know what type of woman you're used to, but I'm not weak-minded or easily intimidated."

Her father had been a master of manipulation, and she'd learned all the tricks.

"You dropped a damned bombshell on me. I'm sorry if I'm not reacting well."

"You were fine at the restaurant. Let's try to go back to that attitude if we can."

"I'll try."

"Then I'll talk to you tomorrow. Please don't follow me."

"I wasn't following you! I just went into the hardware store for some damned plumber's putty!"

"Okay, and while we're at it, you might consider cutting down on your cussing. It's not going to be cute when Peter starts talking and learning words we'd rather he didn't use."

Cal's eyes narrowed. "Any more instructions?"

"No, I think that just about covers it. For now."

"I'll talk to you tomorrow." It was a demand, but she let it go. He was angry, and jealous, although he wouldn't admit it.

"Yes, tomorrow. I have a lot of things to consider. Believe me, most of all, I'll think about what's best for Peter."

"What's best is for a son to know his father and to live in a family with both parents."

Not always. Especially not if the father was acting like an ass. "There are many ways for Peter to get to know you. Living at your ranch, married or not, is only one of the options."

"It's best for everyone."

"No, I think you believe it's best for *you*, but you have to ask yourself if you really want to live in the same house with a woman you don't seem to like very much, much less be married to her."

"I liked you just fine in Fort Worth!"

"I liked you that weekend, too. Right now, however, I'm not so sure."

His eyes narrowed again. "I'm only trying to be responsible. We made that baby together."

"Yes, but I carried him for nine months and went through fourteen hours of labor. Don't tell me it's the same."

"I didn't say it was equal, just that we're in it together."

"I'll get back to you on that," she said, before turning and walking into Toni's office.

CAL RESISTED THE URGE to slam the door as he left Toni's office. He looked up and realized he was just across the street from his attorney's office. What better time to find out his legal rights?

"Oh, hello, Cal," Caroline Brody said as she gathered her purse and closed her desk drawer. "Welcome home."

"Thanks, Mrs. Brody. Is James in?"

"He is. He has an appointment at three o'clock, though."

"I just need a few minutes."

"Hey, Cal," James said, coming out of his office. "Come on in. Mom, I'll see you tomorrow."

"Bye now." Caroline smiled and waved on her way out.

Cal let out a deep breath. "I need some information."

"Okay. Have a seat," James said, motioning to the chairs in his office.

Cal knew next to nothing about parental rights. And he'd better think about prenup agreements, too. He didn't want Christie to think he was after her money, but most of all, he didn't want her to have any rights to the Rocking C, in case their relationship didn't work out.

His father and mother hadn't made their marriage work, even with two children and a ranch to consider. Christie still had her place in Fort Worth, so who knew when she might take off with the baby. She didn't have a good reason to stay. Not yet, anyway. Marriage would bind them together...at least long enough for him to get to know his son.

Seeing her talking to Leo Casale on the sidewalk in front of Toni's office had caused something to snap inside him. She'd called it jealousy, but he didn't think that was it. He was simply clear on what he wanted for the mother of his son. She shouldn't be subject to the advances of some good-looking guy who was attracted to a classy blonde.

And what would happen if she left? Would he have any

rights to the baby? The idea of not being a part of his son's life gave Cal a hollow feeling inside that couldn't be filled by anything—his ranch, friends, family or community.

"Tell me about what you need," James said, snapping Cal back to the present. And his most pressing problem.

"I need to know if I have legal rights to my son."

WHEN CAL ARRIVED at the ranch later in the afternoon, Troy and Raven were in the master bedroom, packing for their move to New Hampshire. Cal stood in the middle of the kitchen and looked at the boxes and bags around the perimeter of the room. Apparently, they'd collected a lot of things in the past year and a half. There were also going-away gifts of hand-labeled jars of jelly and fruit, crocheted scarves and fresh vegetables from friends and neighbors.

Troy had told him that Raven had driven to Texas in her aging Volvo wagon, Pickles, which had been filled with everything from goat cheese to organic flea shampoo for dogs. Apparently Troy had tried to resist her vegetarian lifestyle and antiranching views, but he hadn't been able to help himself and had fallen in love with the Yankee farmer. Raven had been hired to restore a heritage garden, and Troy had been anticipating the arrival of an expert on traditional ranching that Cal had requested from the Cattleman's Association. Somehow, through a merged database mix-up, Troy had gotten the vegetarian and the ranch expert had never shown up.

How his brother could even consider moving to New England was a complete mystery. Troy had obviously lost his mind when he'd fallen for Raven. Not that she wasn't pretty and nice and smart. But really, what self-respecting Texan committed to living in New Hampshire? For all of Troy's odd ideas about the Rocking C, ranching was in his blood. Four generations of Crawford men had raised cattle on this property.

Not chickens and bison and dairy cows. Almost all the Herefords were gone. Thankfully, Troy hadn't sent all of the breeding stock to the auction or the feed lot. A few of the handful of cows left were descended from the original 1880s herd, which meant that Cal could resurrect the Crawford tradition. It might take him a while, but he would rebuild the Rocking C into a Hereford cattle ranch.

As soon as he solved the problem of his son.

"We're just about packed. We'll be on the road first thing in the morning," Troy said, stepping into the room.

"Long drive," Cal said, glancing around, wondering if all this stuff would fit in Troy's SUV.

"We were thinking it would be good to go to Dewey's for dinner. Are you up for that?"

"Sounds good." He'd been there for lunch, but he could go again and get a nice juicy steak. Maybe relax with old friends and family without the distraction of Christie's beautiful face or Peter's drooling smiles. After all, his only brother—albeit the brother who'd played havoc with the ranch—was leaving town. "Is anyone else coming?"

"I'm not sure. Raven might have invited some of her friends."

Was Christie a friend of Raven's? She had mentioned talking to Troy's fiancée, but surely they weren't friends. He hoped not. He needed time to think. Besides, tonight should be about saying goodbye to his brother.

"There's one more thing I wanted to ask you about," Troy said.

Cal felt himself tense, then tried to relax. Not all questions meant trouble. How much more could a man deal with after being home from a war for just over a day? "What?"

"Raven and I thought about taking her dog, Riley—that is,

the stray she found here—back to New Hampshire with us, but we talked it over and decided that he'd probably be happier right here on the Rocking C. How do you feel about keeping him? He's a pretty decent cow dog, plus he's good company."

Cal shrugged. He didn't usually keep a dog. They'd had border collies when he was a kid, but after they'd died, and his dad was gone, Cal had never gotten any more.

"Maybe. He seems okay."

"Raven will miss him like crazy, but there's no sense taking him across the country when he considers this his home now."

"Damn, Troy, you sound like one of those animal rights activists. Since when do *dogs* get to decide where they want to live?"

His brother had the decency to look a little embarrassed but not enough, in Cal's opinion. A man should be in charge of his home, his ranch. A *dog* shouldn't be making decisions.

"I'm just trying to find the best thing for everyone, two-legged or four."

"Yeah, well, I have one important question for the dog."

"What's that?"

"How does he feel about kids? In particular, babies?"

Troy frowned. "Babies? What does that have to do with staying on the ranch?"

"Because—" Cal said, standing up and crossing his arms over his chest "—I found out earlier today that I'm a daddy. I have a son."

Troy looked as shocked as Cal had been earlier. "A son? What, overseas? You've been gone for a year and a half."

"He's nine months old. He…um, well, he was conceived the weekend before I shipped out."

"That weekend you went to Fort Worth?"

"Yeah."

"The blonde you told me about?"

He hadn't told Troy *that* much. "Christie Simmons."

Troy took in a deep breath. "So that's why she showed up here. What does she want, money?"

Cal shook his head. "She said she doesn't want money. Doesn't need it. She's rich."

"What does she want?"

"She says she just wants me to know the boy. Peter is his name."

"Did she know that's your middle name?"

"Yeah, middle name. She didn't name him like she should. He ought to be Calvin Peter Crawford V. Instead, he's Peter Simmons Crawford. Sound like a real yuppie."

"Hey, she named him Crawford. That's a lot more than some women would have done."

"It's not enough. Not nearly enough." He felt his jaw clench as his anger returned. "She should have let me know. He's already nine months old!"

"Did she give you a reason?"

"She gave me a handful, but they don't matter. The fact is that I should have known about my own son."

"Er, are you sure he's yours?"

"I'm sure. You can take one look and see that he's a Crawford. Besides, she offered to have the tests done."

"Wow, a son. I'm an uncle," Troy said, suddenly grinning.

"Don't get too excited. You're leaving, remember?"

The smile faded a little. "I know, but it's not like we're on another planet. Besides, we'll all be getting together next month for the wedding, right?"

"That's right." Although Cal wasn't sure how he could get away from the ranch for a long weekend in Florida to swim with the dolphins or some such nonsense. Why couldn't Raven have a nice little wedding in her nice little town in New Hampshire instead of a "destination wedding" at a "green resort"?

Even if he could get away to attend the festivities, Christie and Peter wouldn't be going to Florida. In a month she'd be knee-deep in renovations on that old motel…if she didn't lose interest and run back to Fort Worth. After he'd insisted they should get married, she might just do that.

He really hadn't handled the concept of "doing the right thing" too well. In hindsight, he shouldn't have spoken while he was still riled over Leo Casale's flirting.

"You look like hell. Is your wound bothering you?" Troy asked.

Cal rubbed his temple. Most of the time, he forgot about the scar. "No, I'm just thinking about Christie's plans. She's renovating the old Sweet Dreams Motel. Crazy idea, if you ask me."

"That place is a disaster. Why would she want to do that?"

"Her family business is hotels. I guess she sees it as a challenge."

"That's a lot of work."

"Toni Casale's company is doing the renovations."

"Well, that's good. Giving the locals some business."

Troy put his hands on his hips and looked around the room. "Damn, there's a lot of stuff here. Too much to deal with tonight. Let's go get a beer and a good Texas steak."

"Ready when you are. I'd just as soon forget about…everything." His brother's departure, all the work that needed to be done to restore the ranch, ensuring a place in his son's life and, last but not least, coexist—married or not—with his son's mother.

"I'll see if Raven is at a stopping point," Troy said as he headed for the doorway leading to the hall. "What should I tell her about Riley?"

Cal closed his eyes and sighed. "Tell her I'll keep the damn dog."

"Hey, if you're going to ignore him, forget it." Troy acted

all indignant. Cal couldn't understand his brother. Falling in love had apparently addled his brain.

"I won't ignore him. If he's good with cattle and children, we'll get along fine."

"I'll tell Raven."

"You do that. I'll meet you at Dewey's."

SHE'D HAD SECOND THOUGHTS when Raven called to invite Christie to attend their bon voyage dinner—because she was a friend of Cal's, Raven had said. Christie wondered how much Raven knew about how "friendly" she and Cal had been in Fort Worth. Or how much they'd been feuding all day. However, she'd decided to accept Raven's invitation, even though she'd just been to Dewey's for lunch. She hadn't been out with adults in so long, and, she admitted to herself, she was curious about Cal's relatives and friends.

She'd dressed in a denim skirt and white blouse with a wide leather belt and strappy sandals with faux turquoise stones set in silver. This was the most Western outfit she could come up with on short notice, and she'd told Raven what she was wearing so the other woman would recognize her.

The parking lot was filling with pickups, Suburbans and Expeditions. Her SRX looked as out of place as she felt when she pulled in next to a big Ford F250. Maybe, if she was going to stay here and renovate the motel, she should get a work vehicle.

But then, she wouldn't be doing much of the actual construction, she thought as she turned off the engine. She'd chosen her vehicle because it was comfortable and safe. She shouldn't get something else just to fit in, just as she wasn't going to change just because people had certain expectations. People like Cal Crawford.

She walked across the asphalt parking lot as the afternoon

heat rose in waves through the only slightly cooler early-evening air. Despite the closed doors and windows, country music drifted across the parking lot. The big red, white and blue sign welcomed her to Dewey's, and the neon beer signs were cheerful beacons in the long shadows. Dewey's looked much different at dinnertime, even before the sun set. Maybe she really needed a night out every now and then.

She entered Dewey's just after a middle-aged couple dressed in starched denim, crisp plaid and straw cowboy hats. They went into the bar area, while Christie looked around the restaurant tables for familiar faces and a black-haired woman.

"Christie!" The familiar female voice came from the far right.

She turned and saw a long table of several people she recognized, and many she didn't. The woman with long black hair must be Raven, and the man beside her resembled Cal, so that must be his brother, Troy.

Toni Casale was also there, along with a few older women Christie recognized from around town, and an older man she hadn't seen before. Another young couple sat across from Raven and Troy. But where was Cal?

"Hi. I guess I'm at the right table."

"I'm so glad you could make it," Raven said. "I know we haven't met in person yet, but I feel as if I know you already. Toni has been telling us about your plans for the old motel." She turned to the others sitting at the table. "Everyone, this is Christie Simmons."

She waved and smiled. "Hello."

Raven leaned close and whispered, "You didn't mention you were gorgeous. You look like a model!"

Christie laughed. "Hardly. I'm a working mother. Well, I'm getting ready to work. I've taken some time off for a career change. And for my son."

"Where is he tonight?" one of the older ladies asked.

"With a babysitter. Toni's niece is watching him. We're staying in Graham." What a stroke of luck to find someone who was experienced and reliable. She'd nearly forgotten what it was like to go out alone.

For the past nine months, she and Peter had been constant companions. Looking into the backseat of the SRX and not seeing his cute little face had seemed odd…and lonely. At least she had her cell phone and Amanda's number so she could call to check on him.

"How old is your child?" another one of the women asked.

She didn't want to tell anyone about Peter until Cal was ready, so she hedged and said, "Still in diapers."

"Well, let me introduce everyone. This is my fiancé, Troy, whom you already know is Cal's brother. And across the table are our newlyweds, James and Sandy Brody." Raven smiled fondly. "She used to go by the name Scarlett, but now she's Sandy. She does wonderful things with hair, just in case you need a cut while you're here, and James is the attorney in town."

Christie thought the man looked at her with a little extra scrutiny. Was he Cal's attorney? Probably. Had Cal talked to him about her…and Peter? Maybe.

"Nice to meet you," she said. Raven then went on to introduce Ida and Rodney Bell, Clarissa Bryant and Bobbi Jean Maxwell.

"I'm sorry my husband, Burl, couldn't be here tonight," Bobbi Jean said. "He's getting over a nasty summer cold or he wouldn't have missed this going-away party."

"It's nice to meet all of you," Christie said, hoping she could remember everyone's names.

Just as the introductions were finished, Christie felt a hand on her shoulder. She spun around to discover Cal standing behind her, a longneck in his other hand and a hat pulled low over his military-short hair. He looked tall, fit and sexy, and her heartbeat increased as she drank him in.

"Christie," he said, his only greeting. After the way they'd parted, she wasn't sure of his mood. She had brushed him off. At that time she hadn't expected to see him again so soon. She wasn't ready to deal with their issues, she realized.

All she wanted was a night out.

"Cal," she replied. Why did he have to be so close? Just the memory of him barging into Toni's office that afternoon made her anxious about being in the same town with him, much less in the same honky-tonk. Not to mention the same house!

She couldn't have imagined that any man would insist two near strangers get married because they'd accidentally made a baby together. A marriage had to be based on more than a child, especially when the mother could provide perfectly well for her baby. She understood why women had needed to get married years and years ago. But not now, not even in a small town with traditional values.

He leaned in close, which must look very intimate to everyone at the table, and whispered in her ear, "Where's the baby?"

"*Peter* is at the motel with a good babysitter," she whispered back, feeling instantly defensive. Cal wasn't interested in *her,* despite his hand on her shoulder and his whispers in her ear. He just wanted to know about his son.

She straightened, smiled and looked at Raven and Troy. "So, when are you actually leaving?"

"Um, tomorrow around noon, probably. We still have to load the SUV," Troy answered.

"Yes, we're taking it to New Hampshire," Raven said with a sigh. "My green Volvo, Pickles, isn't quite up to the trip, so she's staying in Texas."

"It's a wonder you made it down here," Troy said with a shake of his head.

"She's very loyal. She wouldn't break down on the road."

Cal snorted. Rudely, in Christie's opinion. He probably didn't think much of women who named their cars. Christie found it delightful to be living in a town with such interesting people…and one sexy, perplexing and stubborn baby-daddy.

"Take a seat," Cal said, which probably seemed like a *request* for him but sounded like an *order* to her ears.

Christie saw that the only chair at the table was right next to him. With a smile plastered in place for everyone else at the gathering, she sat down. She did not want to take the focus off the going-away party atmosphere for Troy and Raven.

"Here are the drinks," the waitress said as she arrived with a tray. She must have just noticed Christie, because she said, "Oh, hi again. Where's your adorable baby?"

"Yes, where is my nephew?" Troy asked with a big grin.

Christie turned to glare at Cal. So, he'd broken the news. Couldn't he have given her some time to adjust? Couldn't they have told everyone together, quite calmly and *in private?*

He shrugged. "I told you I wasn't keeping it a secret."

"I know that, but…I didn't think you'd blurt it out for everyone like this."

"Why? I'm not ashamed. Besides, Troy's my only brother." He turned to his family and friends. "Just so we're clear, I want everyone to know that I've already asked Christie, the mother of my son, to marry me."

"Good move!" Twila said.

"Congratulations," James Brody said to Cal.

"You most certainly did not!" Christie said, feeling outraged and flushed at his pompous tactics.

Cal narrowed his eyes, just as he'd done this afternoon. "I did, too. Right in Toni's office."

"No, you did not *ask.* And I most certainly didn't agree to any such foolishness!"

"It's not foolish to do the right thing."

"We are not having this argument again."

Rodney Bell chuckled. "You two sure do argue like a married couple already."

Chapter Four

"Rodney! That's none of our business," his wife, Ida, said.

"Cal, you should have asked in a more romantic spot than Toni's office," Raven said gently.

"That's where we were when it occurred to me," he replied.

"Over a wet diaper, a squirming infant and a package of baby wipes," Christie said, deciding to bolster support for her side.

"Oh, that's not good," Clarissa Bryant observed.

"No, not good at all," Sandy Brody said.

At least the women understood. "I'm not getting married because we have a child together," Christie reiterated.

Christie heard Bobbi Jean Maxwell whisper to Ida Bell, "I thought she was a widow."

"Stubborn woman," Cal grumbled as he unrolled his napkin, then snapped it across his lap.

"Stubborn man," Christie answered, reaching for her own rolled napkin and flatware.

"Well," Raven said to Troy, "I guess we're leaving Brody's Crossing about the time things get very interesting."

He smiled. "Looks that way. We can always come to visit…and mediate."

"Bring bandages," Christie said under her breath. If Cal kept up his overbearing ways, he'd need them.

They ordered dinner and managed to remain civil throughout the meal. Raven and Troy seemed to have a good time, although they got nostalgic with their friends about all the things that had happened since Raven had temporarily—and accidentally—moved to Texas over a year ago.

Christie declined another beer and was thinking about leaving when Cal grabbed her hand. "Let's dance," he said as he pulled back her chair. She was so surprised she went along with him.

There was no band on this weeknight, but country-western songs came through the speakers in the bar and dance area. The rustic wood enclosed them as Cal led her onto a floor scuffed by thousands of boots.

Without a word, he led her into a fast two-step. Fortunately, she'd danced at Billy Bob's and Gilley's, so she kept up with his quick pace.

"You're a good dancer," he said close to her ear as they danced straight down the length of the floor.

"Thanks. You're pretty good yourself. I don't guess you got much practice while you were in the military."

"Hardly." He slowed as the music transitioned into a song Christie recognized was by the Dixie Chicks. "Come out to the ranch tomorrow," he said.

"Was that a request or an order?" Cal really needed to work on his people skills. He wasn't still in the army, and she definitely wasn't a ranch hand.

He sighed. "Sorry. What I meant was that I'd like for you to see the ranch. I got to thinking that you can't make a decision on where to live until you see the house."

"Good point. I have an appointment with a Realtor in the morning, but I could come after lunch."

"Are you taking the baby on the appointment?"

"Yes. I only have a babysitter for tonight. Actually, this is the first time I've been out in a long time."

He seemed to consider that as he turned them through the corner. His arm tightened and she brushed against his chest. She almost apologized, which seemed ridiculous since they'd made a baby together. In many ways, though, he was a stranger. He even looked different, with his more serious demeanor and the scar at his temple. The wound was an outward reminder that he'd been gone, serving his country, risking his life.

While she'd been home, giving birth to his baby and wondering about how to break the news. "I'd love to come to the ranch tomorrow after Peter's nap. I'll bring him, and we can spend the afternoon."

He seemed surprised, but then he nodded and said, "Good."

They finished the slow dance without speaking again. She tried to relax and enjoy the music and the man, but he made her too nervous. Christie wanted to protect herself and, most especially, Peter. She had to do what was best for all of them.

But what was best? Maybe she'd find out tomorrow.

Everyone was talking as she and Cal returned to the table. As Christie excused herself to go to the ladies' room before leaving for the drive to Graham, she was surprised when Raven joined her.

"I wanted to speak to you alone before we leave tomorrow," Raven said. "Cal isn't happy with the Rocking C as it is now, even though it was beginning to fail before he left for active duty. When I came to Texas last year, Troy was worried sick about the place. The bank loan was coming due with no hope of making enough from the sale of the cattle. Truly, the ranch could have been lost."

"That's terrible. But apparently you and Troy turned it around."

"Mostly Troy. Cal doesn't like the choices his brother made, though, and that hurts Troy because he did what was necessary to save the ranch." Raven sighed. "If Cal tries to revert to the way it was, the same problems will arise. Lack of diversity in a competitive market, paying the going rate for hay, no other source of income. At least now he has revenue coming in from the free-range chicken and dairy-cow leases. And he has a built-in market for the bison meat, as sad as I am to think about animals going to slaughter. At least the butcher shop here uses more humane methods than those horrible feed lots."

"I don't know anything about ranching and very, very little about cattle," Christie said.

"You don't have to know about ranching to help him. He told Troy that he's going to change the ranch back to Herefords, but I've noticed there are other, more important matters on his mind."

"What's that?"

"Now that he has Peter to consider—and his relationship with you, of course—he hasn't had time to think about the Rocking C."

"Are you sure about that?"

"Definitely. And I have a big favor to ask," Raven said, placing her hand on Christie's arm. "Keep him busy. Don't let him try to change the ranch."

"Raven, I'm not sure I can do that."

"I'm just asking you to try. Or at least don't encourage him. Troy has worked hard to save the Rocking C. Cal just doesn't see that yet. He's all tied up in the past."

"He's very traditional."

"Yes, he is. There must be a reason, but I don't know him well enough to figure out why."

Christie sighed. "I don't, either."

"Please, get to know him. Help him. I have a feeling you're the only one who can."

"That's a heavy burden," she said.

"I'm sorry, but this is important. To all of us, I think. I love Troy so much. I don't want him to believe that all his work was in vain and that Cal will eventually lose the ranch because he's hardheaded."

"I can't promise, but I'll see what I can learn about the ranch. Other than that, I'm not sure…"

"That's all I can hope for. I've been gone from my farm far too long. I've depended on friends to take care of things in New Hampshire and it's been a lot of work for them. Plus, I miss my family, friends and animals so much. I'm lucky that Troy offered to move to my home. Still, I feel so bad, going off and leaving Cal when he's just gotten back. But somehow, I feel that he needs time to himself. He harbors so much anger. And inside, I think there is a great amount of sadness."

"I don't know." Raven's observations made Christie wonder—did Cal hold secrets close to his heart? Could he be suffering from more than an obvious war wound?

As she walked back to the table, she thought about how complicated her life had gotten in the past two days. She needed to reconcile Cal's getting to know Peter with his stubborn insistence they needed to "do the right thing"; she needed to get started on renovating the Sweet Dreams Motel; and now, she needed to discover how to help the Crawford family by keeping Cal from changing the ranch back to how it was before he left for military service. Oh, and to do that last one, she needed to find out what made Cal sad or angry or moody.

She'd always prided herself on being independent, but this time, she might have bitten off a little more than she could chew.

CAL WAVED GOODBYE TO TROY and Raven, then immediately went to work on changes to the ranch. He tried to ignore the advice on bison that Troy had given him, along with a notebook from the breeder and former owner. Be calm around them. No working them with horses. Don't crowd them, especially the bull. To Cal, the idea of raising the native animals was fine—for someone else. But they didn't belong on the Rocking C.

In a pasture close to the house—one not inhabited by bison, chickens or dairy cows—he milled among the small herd of Herefords, the dog called Riley at his side. These cows behaved as ranch animals should, frightened but not panicked. He could work them on horseback, and if he went into their pasture, they didn't try to kill him. The bison bull, on the other hand, gave him the evil eye whenever they crossed paths.

He created a list of the heifers' ear-tag numbers. Later, he'd look them up on the database he'd created a long time ago from the ranch breeding records. His father had written these out longhand in a spiral notebook long before personal computers.

He had to admit the fences and outbuildings were in better shape than before he'd gone overseas. With just him and two ranch hands, he hadn't had time for nonemergency maintenance. There had been no need for paint on the old buildings, and he'd never minded the weeds in the yard or thought about planting flowers around the house. Someone had taken care of those things, though, and as nice as it looked, he wouldn't be keeping up frivolous improvements. As long as the cattle had feed and water and the house had heat in the winter, he could manage just fine.

How about Christie and the baby? his conscience asked. *Will they be "fine" with the way things are?* It didn't matter because, right now, the place looked female-friendly. With Christie's independent attitude, who knew how long she'd be there? He could only hope to convince her that they needed to get married. Then she could do whatever she wanted, within reason, of course.

Just about the time he stepped past the flowers by the back

steps and entered the freshly painted yellow mudroom, he heard the crunch of gravel as someone drove up the driveway. The vehicle stopped and he felt his heart rate increase and his stomach clench. Somewhere in the yard, the dog started barking. Turning and looking out the back door, he verified that, yes, Christie and his son had arrived.

Her shiny, platinum-colored car looked out of place on this ranch. Of course, if she'd pulled up before his brother and Raven had fixed it up, she would have probably turned around and left since the ranch had looked considerably rougher, more rural and less appealing to a city girl.

"Riley, hush!" he yelled at the dog.

The driver's door opened and Christie emerged in skinny jeans and a hot-pink shirt tied at her waist. Double damn. She looked as hot as Texas in August. She sure didn't look like a woman who'd given birth nine months ago...or ever. If she'd changed one bit from the time he'd known her a year and a half ago, he couldn't tell where. Especially not in those tight jeans, he thought as she opened the back car door and leaned in.

Snapping out of his thoughts, he walked toward her to help get the baby and all the gear she carried. Who knew one baby needed so much stuff? Riley followed, sniffing Christie's feet and the tires of the Cadillac.

Cal watched her bend and wiggle while she unlatched Peter. The woman still turned him on, even though he was perturbed about the decisions she'd made. He wanted to think his attraction to her made no sense, but, unfortunately, it made perfect sense. He had excellent memories of their time together. He hadn't been with another woman since that weekend in Fort Worth. And one look at Christie Simmons would make any man forget a reason for being angry about anything.

She straightened and put her finger to her lips. Then she lifted the baby out of the car seat. His head, covered in short, fine, light brown hair, flopped onto Christie's shoulder while his little fist curved right against her breast.

Lucky little baby.

Cal reached in and snagged the diaper bag, then followed Christie into the house, the dog on her heels. Cal held the back door for her as she walked through the utility room into the kitchen.

"Do you want to sit down in the living room?" Cal asked in a whisper. "Or would you rather lay him down on a bed?"

"He could roll right off a regular bed. I'd rather put him on the couch until he wakes up, which should be soon."

He led the way into the living room, which was just a few steps from the kitchen. At least Troy and Raven hadn't touched his thirty-two-inch TV, housed in an equally large oak entertainment center. And his favorite recliner, while slightly more used by Troy, still faced the big screen.

Christie settled on the couch and lay Peter beside her on the cushion. He immediately rolled toward the back but didn't wake up. The dog sat at Christie's feet and stared at her, his bushy tale wagging as if she were his new best friend.

"So," he said, feeling unusually awkward, "this is obviously the living room."

"It's a good size," she said, looking around. "Is there also a family room or a den?"

"No, this is it. There are three bedrooms and an office, and two bathrooms. Just a typical one-story ranch-style home." Of course, it wasn't typical for Christie, who had probably grown up in a mansion. "My father had the house built in the seventies, when I was just a little older than—" he nodded toward the sleeping baby "—Peter."

"Oh? Is there another house on the property?"

"Not anymore. The house my father grew up in was torn down. It had major foundation problems. The remains of the house before that, the original homestead, is just beyond a hill out back."

"How about a bunkhouse?"

He shook his head. "Not habitable. The roof caved in on one corner after a tree blew over in a windstorm, years ago. The two ranch hands don't live on the Rocking C. They both have families in the area."

"I see."

"Look, Christie. If you move in, you'd be living here. There's no other house. We'd be under the same roof."

"I just wanted to make sure what the situation was."

"I guess that depends on what you found out this morning." He felt tension building as he watched her, as she obviously didn't want to be there or think about living there. With him. "Any luck finding a suitable place to live?"

"Not really. Both houses needed a lot of work, heavy cleaning and baby-proofing."

"Baby-proofing?"

"Latches on cabinets, safety gates, electrical outlet covers. Things like that."

Cal had heard of these things on a home-improvement show he sometimes watched, but he'd never known anyone who actually used them. Of course, he wasn't close to anyone who had a baby.

"It's important to keep the baby safe," she added.

"Funny how most of us grew up just fine without those gadgets, yet now they are essential. Hell, Troy and I were out in the barn and running around the property as soon as we could shove on a pair of boots."

Christie looked shocked at that observation, but she didn't say his parents were negligent or crazy. "Times change, I suppose. The baby book has a long list of things necessary to baby-proof a house."

"If it makes you feel better, I'll do it."

"The point is, if it will make Peter safer, *we* should do it."

He frowned. "I said I'd do it, and I will."

She nodded, glancing at the baby. "How about the dog?"

"Riley? He was a stray Raven brought to the ranch a year ago. She said he was good-natured. There was a note on a homemade collar, and Raven said it looked as if it had been written by a child, asking someone to find a good home for Riley." Cal shrugged. "So Raven thought the dog should stay here."

Christie reached down and stroked Riley's black-and-brown head, making him wiggle like a puppy. "He seems very sweet. We'll have to see how he reacts to Peter."

"He's gentle with chickens and calves, if that means anything."

"I have no idea," she said, continuing to pet the dog. "I never had a dog growing up, but I planned to get a yellow Lab as soon as I settled in a house."

He wondered if she meant there, in Brody's Crossing, or back in Fort Worth. Or someplace else. As much as he thought they should get married for Peter's sake, as much as she talked about buying and renovating the old motel, he just couldn't see her living there forever.

"If you want another dog, we could work that out."

"I'll keep that in mind," she said, glancing at the baby.

"Does that mean you're going to move in here?"

"I'd like to see the rest of the house," she said.

"Like the bedrooms?" Like where she would be sleeping? Not with him, he was pretty sure she'd insist. And in all fairness, although he wanted her on a very physical level, he had to admit there was an awkwardness about their situation that should be overcome before they started anything. Like sex.

"Yes. And the bathroom I'd be using."

"As soon as he wakes up, I'll finish the tour. Then you can decide if the house is good enough for you and the baby."

"It's not a question of 'good enough,'" Christie insisted. "It's about whether we can make this work with Peter's things and my clothes and everything else that goes into living arrangements."

Whatever she said, he'd still know that this house wasn't anywhere near as big or nice as what she was used to. "Well, I'm ready for some coffee. Want some?"

"Do you have a diet soda?"

"Do I look like a diet soda kind of guy? Because if I do, I'm gonna need to be the 'before' of one those straight-guy makeovers."

She rolled her eyes. "I'm just asking. I thought Raven might have left some."

"No, she only drinks organic juice, filtered water and stuff like that. Soda is way too processed for her."

"Water will be fine."

He nodded and walked out of the room. Water. She probably expected some fancy bottled kind. On the Rocking C, you got it straight from the tap.

CHRISTIE ARRIVED at the Rocking C three days later, her SRX loaded with suitcases and baby stuff, food and bottled water. She'd also made arrangements for a few deliveries that afternoon.

She hoped Cal didn't mind.

Since he wanted her to move in, though, she figured he wouldn't care if she made the house more comfortable and functional. The houses she'd looked at would have all needed considerably more upgrades than Cal's home. She could never let Peter crawl around on soiled carpet and dirty, dingy vinyl tiles. The bathrooms were cramped and old, and all the owners wanted longer-term commitments than she required.

She'd even considered buying a manufactured home and putting it on a lot, except there were no lots ready and she would have been stuck in the suite at Graham for weeks and weeks. At that point, she realized she was running scared— running from the idea of sharing a house with Cal. She was acting as if they weren't two rational adults who'd created a baby together. They might have been lovers once, and okay, she was still attracted to Cal, but that didn't mean they had to act on their desires. She could control herself, and she was sure that Cal, with his tendency toward self-restraint and his military training, could keep his hands to himself.

And really, they were supposed to be focusing on Peter, giving father and son a chance to bond. What better way to do that than be in the same house together?

"Ba-ba-ba," Peter demanded, banging his rattle on the hard plastic part of the car seat.

"Yes, baby, I know. I'm going to get your bottle fixed as soon as we get these things into the house."

He started to cry as she grabbed four plastic bags of perishable food from the back, perched him on her hip and looped his diaper bag on her other shoulder. "Mommy's hurrying," she muttered, trying to sound soothing but probably failing as he continued to fuss.

The dog ran up, wagging his tail. "Look, Peter. A doggy." At least Riley had the sense to stay out from under her feet. Maybe he and Peter could become good friends.

"Hey, I'll help with that," she heard Cal say as she swayed like an overburdened donkey toward the back door. She really should see about getting a nanny.

Suddenly the plastic grocery bags and the heavy diaper bag were lifted from her. Even Peter stopped fussing and stared at Cal. "Thanks. I was in a hurry to fix him a bottle."

"I wasn't sure what time you were going to be here," Cal said as he opened the back door for her.

She walked through to the kitchen and turned to face him. Wow. He looked great, in a totally grubby cowboy way. His tan hat, pulled low on his forehead, shaded his blue-gray eyes. A pale blue chambray shirt, unbuttoned at the throat, was dampened by sweat on his chest and around the collar. His jeans were dusty, worn and fit him like a fine leather glove.

"Yeah, I know I'm a mess," he said. "I'll try not to get the baby dirty."

"Peter," she said, her voice slightly breathless as she looked away. "His name is Peter."

"I know his name," Cal said, placing the grocery bags on the counter. As he brushed by her to put the diaper bag on the table, she inhaled a big whiff of hot cowboy. This was a different side of Cal, one she hadn't thought about. Men she'd dated in the past had had office jobs. They'd smelled like subtle, expensive cologne, leather and money. The only time they'd sweat was when they worked out, played polo or spent the day at the lake.

"You've got a full load out there," he said, turning toward her and placing his hands on his hips. "Do you want all of it in your bedroom?" The bedroom she'd share with Peter, not Cal.

"I don't think it will all fit. The bigger baby toys and the bouncy seat need to go in the family room."

"That would be the room with my recliner and big TV?"

"Um, that's right. As you told me, it's the only living area in the house." She paused while looking through the diaper bag for one of Peter's bottles. "And the high chair, of course, goes in the kitchen."

"Sure. I'll get it unloaded and if you need help moving it around, I'll do that later."

"If you could get the portable bed in first, that would be great. Peter will probably want a nap after his bottle."

Cal went off to unload her SUV. She sighed as she watched his dusty, worn jeans disappear through the door. They sure caressed a nice butt. She'd remembered that from their weekend together, and the evidence was still there, right before her eyes.

She sighed as she settled into a chair and filled Peter's bottle. "Your daddy is one hot cowboy," she whispered to her son. "Unfortunately, he has a temper to match."

While she fed Peter, Cal made multiple trips to the Cadillac to bring in all of her things. She hadn't realized she'd accumulated so much. Maybe now wasn't the time to tell Cal how much more she planned to bring into his house.

When he finished, he went to the sink and filled a glass of water. She watched him drink, then looked away. What was wrong with her? She should be thinking about where to put all the baby things, not remembering how she'd gotten into this situation in the first place.

"The plastic things are sure colorful," Cal commented.

"I know. The manufacturers apparently think that bright red, yellow, blue and green go with every decor."

"Since this house is mostly beige, I guess it doesn't matter much. Beige goes with everything, right?"

"I suppose." This house was dated and boring, but she didn't want to say anything negative because she figured his late mother must have chosen the colors and style. She knew that happened sometimes when a loved one was gone. Christie's grandfather hadn't wanted to change one single thing in his house after her grandmother had passed away.

"Speaking of style, I have a meeting in Fort Worth next week with a designer who has a lead on fabric and vinyl for the motel. Do you know of anyone who might want to babysit Peter during the day? I'm probably going to be in and out of meetings with suppliers, and it's difficult for him. I'd ask Toni's niece, but she works during the day."

"I don't know." He refilled his glass and drank more water. "I suppose you could ask Ida Bell or Bobbi Jean Maxwell. Both those ladies know almost everyone around here."

"Yes, I met both of them the other night. Do you have their phone numbers?"

"Sure. We can call them later."

"Good. Um, there's just one more thing I should mention."

"What's that?" he asked as he set his glass in the sink.

"I took the liberty of ordering a few things I thought might be necessary now that I'm moving in. I've made arrangements for delivery, and of course I've paid for them, but in case you see some trucks coming onto the property, I wanted you to know."

"Things? What kind of things?"

"Oh, just some necessities. A crib for Peter, for example. Some baby gates so we can keep him out of rooms where he could hurt himself. Oh, and a new refrigerator."

"A what!"

"Well, yours is rather small, and I needed more room for Peter's formula, juice and food. Plus, I need some room for my food. I measured first, of course, to make sure it would fit."

"We should have talked this over."

"Yes, you're right, but you've been busy and so have I." In fact, she'd made great progress with the renovations. Already the debris and an unapproved storage room addition had been hauled away. The roofing materials would be delivered on Monday, and repairs to the vintage concrete-block structures and walls would begin immediately.

She and Toni were meeting tomorrow to discuss the pros and cons of installing a microwave, small refrigerator and coffeemaker into each unit. Personally, Christie loved the convenience of appliances in a hotel or motel room. Of course, they weren't vintage, so they'd have to be hidden. She wanted the visuals to be perfect. When a guest walked into the room, she wanted them to believe they were stepping back in time.

"What did you plan to do with my old appliances? Throw them out? Are you leaving the new stuff here even if you don't stay?"

"I'll leave them for you when, or if, I move out. We can consider them compensation for the deposit and rent I would have paid if I'd rented a house, okay? That's reasonable, since I didn't buy high-end stainless. I tried to get appliances that would match what you already had."

"Nice of you to think of aesthetics," he said with a little bite of sarcasm. "As if I care about appliances matching."

"Well, I care, and you'd be surprised how disruptive mismatched items can be to your senses." Hmm, rather like a stubborn rancher and an equally opinioned woman, she thought. Perhaps she was being unrealistic, imagining they could live together, but she had to try for Peter's sake.

Cal rolled his eyes. "Any other changes you have planned for my house?"

Peter had finished his bottle, so Christie placed him on her shoulder as she had when he was a much smaller baby. "You know, for someone who insisted I should move in here and even wanted me to marry him, you're quick to remind me this is *your* house."

He took a deep breath and looked down at his scuffed boots. "You're right. It's not easy thinking about someone else living with me. It's kind of hard since my brother and Raven were here for nearly a year and a half. I had to give over my ranch to Troy, and he changed it all."

"Not all, surely. The house appears to be…well, it doesn't look recently updated. And it's still a ranch, right?"

"It's not the same kind of ranch," he said, looking up, his eyes bright. "Troy sold off almost all the Herefords and signed

contracts with dairy-cow farmers, free-range-chicken pro-
ducers and bison-meat providers that I can't do a damn thing
about for two years! Most of those animals aren't *mine*. Troy
made those changes even when he knew I didn't want him to."

She stood up and placed a hand on Cal's sleeve. "A lot
has happened in the past week. Coming home to the Rocking
C, finding me here, discovering you have a son. It's so much
to take in."

"I can handle it," he said, sounding defensive.

"I know you can, but it must be hard. I'm not trying to
make things worse, but I'm probably going to make mistakes.
I'm not accustomed to running my decisions by someone
else, either. At least, not in a long time. Even when I was
married before, we maintained a lot of our own interests. And
he was perfectly willing for me to make decisions about our
apartment in Paris and house in Italy."

"Yeah, well, I'm not your first husband, and I need to be
consulted before you make major changes. It's not that I want
to say no, but this is something we should decide together."

"You're right."

Cal nodded and walked off. Christie sighed. No, he wasn't
anything like Aldo Amalfi. And despite the way Cal looked in
jeans and a cowboy hat and the fact he wanted to be involved
in their baby's life, he wasn't going to be her next and *last*
husband, either, unless they could learn to compromise.

Chapter Five

Cal retreated to the office to make a new database of his extremely reduced herd. Just the numbers on the heifers' ear tags couldn't tell the history of the Rocking C, nor could they show how much struggle went into forcing a living out of the land every year.

His father and grandfather had told stories of the early years of the ranch. Even during the Great Depression and throughout various droughts, their Herefords had survived. Cattle had taken care of the family when the family took care of the cattle, Grandpa Crawford had always said. While other ranches had come and gone, the Rocking C had survived.

His father hadn't loved ranching so much as he'd lived it. They'd never been wealthy, not like some families who'd drilled for oil on their property or sold off acreage when times got tough, but they'd gotten by, with some years better than others. There must be a gene in some families that formed that kind of bond with the land and animals. Troy didn't have the gene.

At one time, Cal had questioned whether he had it. In the days immediately after his father's accident, he'd felt unworthy of carrying on the tradition. He had been only twenty years old when his father had died. A scared twenty-year-old responsible for his kid brother, a ranch and all the Crawford heritage.

He'd learned and stayed true to the family traditions until the other requirement for Crawford males—military service—had taken him away. His father and grandfather had told him that they'd gotten through active duty in Vietnam and World War II with the knowledge that they'd return, God willing, to a place unchanged by war. That thought had comforted them, but Cal had come back to a ranch he barely recognized, at least beyond the barns and pastures.

And now Christie was bringing new things into the house. A new refrigerator. Baby furniture. A new washer and dryer, she'd later revealed. Once she spent a night in the guest bedroom, she'd probably order one of those fancy mattresses that cost a few thousand.

He put his head between his hands and stared at the desk. The nice, quiet, simple life he wanted was disappearing more and more every day. Some people might ask what they'd done wrong to deserve this chaos, but Cal knew.

He knew exactly what he'd done, and his transgression had nothing to do with Christie or Troy.

AFTER CHRISTIE CALLED Bobbi Jean Maxwell the next morning, she was invited to lunch with the "the girls" at the café in town. Bobbi Jean was sure that they could find a suitable babysitter for Peter. In fact, she seemed to have someone in mind. After checking to make sure the other women didn't mind a baby joining them, she discovered she was looking forward to creating new friendships.

The new appliances came promptly at ten o'clock, long after Cal was out doing whatever he did on the ranch, and while Peter was having his midmorning snack of an apple cereal bar and juice in his sippy cup, which he seemed determined to use as a missile.

Christie had the delivery men place the old refrigerator in

an extra room in the barn, where Cal had indicated he'd use it for beer and vaccines. That didn't seem like a good combination to Christie, but that was his business. The outdated washer and dryer were donated to a local charity since Cal had no other use for them.

She rushed to get herself and Peter ready for lunch in town. He seemed a little fussy. Perhaps he was cutting a new tooth, since he was also drooling. It would be so nice to have someone else she could rely on to watch Peter while she took more than a quick shower or applied a minimum of makeup.

Even while she'd lived in Fort Worth, her mother and friends hadn't stepped in to care for the baby. Christie hadn't realized how little her mother knew about children. After all, she'd had a bilingual nanny so her mother could pursue her own interests and tell herself that her daughter was better off with a "professional."

That was one reason Christie was reluctant to hire a nanny. Would doing so mean she was more like her mother than she wanted to admit? Was she selfish to want time to herself? She didn't think so, but she wondered about the old motel. The project was important to her. Renovating the Sweet Dreams would give her something productive to do, even if doing it while caring for Peter might prove challenging.

She and Peter drove into town, making a small detour to drive by the motel. Sure enough, there was a crew at work on the roof, and another man was scraping the rusty metal railings along the parking lot. Smiling, she continued down the main street to the establishment that was simply named "Café."

"That's very quaint," she told Peter as she parked the car across the street.

Inside, she joined Bobbi Jean Maxwell, Clarissa Bryant and Ida Bell in a booth. The waitress brought a wooden high chair for Peter and placed him at the end of the Formica table.

"We're so glad you could come to lunch," Clarissa said. "Raven had lunch with us regularly, and we're going to miss her."

"Your baby is adorable," Ida said.

"I think he's teething," she explained as Peter began to fuss. While she chatted with the ladies, he alternately stuffed crackers and the teething ring into his mouth, making a big mess.

"Renovations are coming along quickly at the motel," Christie told the ladies. "I really feel that I need to be there more often, plus make some buying trips to Fort Worth or Wichita Falls."

"Of course you do. You can't drag a baby all over the place all the time. Why, he'd never get a nap!" Ida said.

"I just feel as if I should be able to take care of him in addition to managing this renovation."

Clarissa waved her hand. "Mothers always feel that way."

"My daughter Darla is a kindergarten teacher during the school year, but she's off for the summer and she's looking for a job. I know you'd want to talk to her, but I can tell you, she'd be just great for what you need." Bobbi Jean smiled. "Of course, I am a proud mother."

"Does she have any children of her own?"

"No! Her low-down husband kept telling her he wanted to wait, then he up and ran off with a video-store clerk in Decatur. Darla is better off without him, of course, but that just riled all of us."

"Yes, I imagine that would. So, is she divorced now?"

"Yes, as of February. She moved back in with us, but she's looking for her own place. That's why she needs extra money."

"I'd love to meet her. Do you think she could come out to the ranch later today or in the morning?"

"I'm sure she can."

"So, are you staying at the Rocking C?" Ida asked.

"Yes, I am, for now. I plan to stay there until the owner's suite I'm preparing for the motel is ready."

"He wants to get married," Ida said.

"Um, yes, but I don't think that's a good idea right now."

"You need to know someone well before you get married. Look at what happened to poor Darla," Bobbi Jean said.

"Oh, but then there's spontaneity," Clarissa said. "Running off with a man could be very exciting."

"Oh, are you speaking from experience?" Ida asked with a grin.

The ladies laughed, then Clarissa explained to Christie, "I've been a widow for so long they think it would be fun to see me act like a silly girl. Well, that's not going to happen, but I do remember the feeling."

Christie remembered spontaneity. Cal had swept her off her feet that weekend in Fort Worth. They'd barely come up for air and food. That didn't mean they were a good match for marriage. And if they weren't…at least she had other options. The motel. Her condo in Fort Worth. Another career in another town. She could do whatever she wanted.

After ordering lunch, Christie gave Bobbi Jean her cell-phone number so Darla could call her. "I hope we can work something out. I think Peter is old enough that he needs to be away from me a little, and the renovations are really speeding right along."

"I hope so, too. Darla needs the money, but most of all, taking care of a baby will keep her mind off her cheating ex and give her something positive to think about."

Christie hoped that didn't mean Darla was so negative now that she couldn't see hope in the future. She couldn't have someone who was actually depressed around Peter. Until she got the house baby-proofed, he would have to be watched carefully. Every time she looked at him, she thought that he was her little miracle. For someone who'd been told she couldn't have children, having this big, healthy baby boy seemed a huge responsibility at times.

The rest of the lunch passed with chitchat about some upcoming events that Christie might want to consider now that she was starting a business in town. As she finished her salad and sweet tea, Christie felt more and more that she'd made the right decision by moving to Brody's Crossing.

Now if she could hire Darla as Peter's nanny for the summer, she would have the time to renovate the motel without worrying about him. Then, on a personal level, all she'd have to be concerned with was her awkward relationship with Cal…and whether she should try to get back the magic of that one, special weekend.

"I DON'T HAVE A CLUE what to do," Cal told Burl Maxwell later that afternoon as they shared a cold beer at the barn.

"Son, you just have to think about the positives. The cash flow, for one thing. The contracts Troy signed give you a guaranteed income for at least two years."

Cal hadn't been thinking of only the ranch, although that was nagging at his conscience all the time. "You know a lot about the Rocking C. Did he talk you into going along with the changes?"

"He didn't have to." Burl took a drink of his light beer. "I could see the need before he came to me. I gave him some suggestions. Some he took, some he didn't."

"You didn't say anything to me before I left."

"You didn't want to hear it. A couple of times Rodney and I tried to bring it up, but you shut us down."

Cal didn't remember specific incidents, but he did recall nixing any suggestion that the Rocking C change drastically. "It's all about the stock," his father used to say, and Cal had tried his best to maintain the best heifers and buy the best bull semen he could to produce a healthy, big steer that would get top dollar. Some years, though, there wasn't any top dollar.

"I couldn't do anything about the market," he said, thinking about the drop in beef prices whenever there was a contamination scare, a glut of imports or a drought that caused ranchers to sell off stock.

"Of course not. None of us can. That's why it's good to be versatile."

"My father would never have put up with dairy cows and free-range chickens running all over his property."

"Your father would have wanted the Rocking C to survive, just like he would have been grateful that you came back from the war in Afghanistan with only a slight wound. It could have been much worse. Think about that."

"I've thought about it every night," Cal said, taking a long pull of beer. If the roadside bomb had gone off seconds earlier, if he hadn't turned to see what his buddy in the passenger seat had said…

"Of course you have. I'm sorry. I didn't mean to say that you don't appreciate your life. It's just that…darn it, Cal, you have to move forward. You've got a lot going for you."

"Yeah, I tell myself that. But you know, I wanted to drive through the gate and see the ranch like I remember it. Like it was before…before everything got so damned complicated."

"You mean before that pretty lady moved to town?"

"Yeah, that, too." He took another drink. "Not that I'm angry I have a son. It's just one more thing that's not right with my life. Peter should be named after me, for one." Cal didn't want to tell Burl, but the baby intimidated him. He wasn't sure what to do or say around him. He wanted to be a father—and he'd always known he needed to have a son—but how did he learn to be a *dad?*

"At least he has your middle name."

Cal shrugged, unwilling to continue thinking about the baby's lack of name heritage. "Christie and I should get married, but that's not happening. Hell, I don't even know what to do to get close to her. It's like we've never met, but obviously, we did."

"Well, that's something I don't have any experience with," Burl said. "Bobbi Jean and I had a more traditional courtship and marriage in a different time. Women all want the same thing, though, I suppose."

"What's that?"

"Well, they want romance," Burl answered, as if it were the most obvious thing in the world.

"I'm a rancher and a former soldier. I don't know a lot about romance."

"How did you knock that pretty girl's socks off in the first place, then?"

"Hell if I know. We were in a bookstore on Sundance Square, standing in line to get coffee. Both of us were holding the same book. I'd gotten the paperback to read while I waited for the long transit. She'd gotten the hardback because…hell, Christie's that kind of person. The 'hardback books on the shelf' kind of person, you know?"

"I think I know what you mean."

"And we started talking, and I bought her a cup of coffee—one of those fancy drinks with whipped cream on top—and we sat down together. The next thing I knew it was Monday morning and I had to get back to the base."

"Sounds like it was something special."

"It was, but now I don't know what I did or how to do it again."

"Back in my day, a first date meant a lot."

"I guess." They'd never had a traditional first date. Suddenly, a lightbulb went off. "I need to ask her out on a date. Maybe bring her some flowers." Instead, he'd been complaining about new appliances she'd purchased and making remarks about all the baby stuff she'd brought into the living room. If he couldn't convince her that he wanted to start over, she'd leave for sure and take his son with her.

"Sounds like a good start," Burl said, taking a long pull of his beer.

WHEN CHRISTIE AND PETER arrived back at the ranch, Peter was fast sleep. She carried him inside and placed him in the newly assembled crib. She hadn't had time to put all of the bedding around the mattress, but there were clean sheets and he didn't require anything but his pacifier to have a nice, long nap.

She settled on the couch in the living room after grabbing her cell phone, BlackBerry and the notes she'd taken on paper while she was out. Cal had said she could use the office, but she didn't need to disturb his cluttered desk. Besides, the overstuffed couch was fairly comfortable.

First she made a phone call to Toni regarding the upcoming trip to purchase more materials, then checked with her condo management to make sure everything was fine back in Fort Worth. She even took a moment to call her mother, telling her that they were staying at a local ranch until the owner's suite was finished. The conversation was brief, cordial and unsatisfying, as usual.

Christie was sure her mother had in mind a grand owner's suite, with ivory swag drapes framing a view of a landscaped pool, a whirlpool tub for two and a California king mattress. Something an SHG property might boast. But Christie didn't want an upscale hotel.

When the renovations were finished, at least she'd have a view of the pool. A small, family-friendly pool painted turquoise, with a vintage concrete fence painted white, coral and lime-green, surrounded by loungers and perhaps a table with a brightly patterned umbrella.

She put that on her list of items to find during her shopping trip next week, saving it in her BlackBerry. Perhaps something in a tropical pattern of fruit—

"Christie?"

She jumped at the sound of Cal's voice, soft as it was. "Oh, hi." He stood in the wide entrance from the living room to the kitchen, a bit worn-looking as though he'd been working outside. He made no move to come into the living room.

"I didn't want to interrupt if you're on the phone or... whatever."

"I just finished. I try to make calls while Peter is sleeping. I'm sure I sound much more professional and coherent then."

"I suppose it's tough trying to do all these renovations and relocating with him being so young."

"I'm not sure there's a good age, but I think it is hard with a baby. He can't do anything for himself."

"Did Bobbi Jean or Ida help you find a babysitter?"

"We'll see. Darla Maxwell is supposed to call me. Do you know her?" Christie had forgotten to ask how old Darla was. If she was close to Cal's age, they might have gone to school together. Or dated. Or more.

"Sure. Not very well. She's a lot younger. Maybe late twenties. I was already running the ranch by the time she got to high school, but our families were always friendly."

Oh, good. He and Darla hadn't been sweethearts or lovers or anything. That might be awkward. "I hope she calls. Bobbi Jean said Darla got a divorce from her cheating husband."

"Yeah, that happens."

Christie didn't know what to say to that. Darla's husband had been cheating, but just as easily, they could have had "irreconcilable differences." All the more reason to be really sure before you took the plunge.

"So, are you finished for the day?"

"Just about, except for nightly chores." He paused and

looked down, then back at her, his eyes intense. "I wanted to say that I'm sorry I've been so…negative this past week. I don't have an excuse other than what I told you before, but still, I shouldn't have acted the way I did or said some of the things I did. I know you're just trying to make the best of things, and I'm glad you have the money to buy what you need to be more comfortable."

That was the longest speech Cal had ever spoken to her. He was usually a man of few words, even when they'd first met. "Um, thank you. I really do understand that all of this is a shock. I'll try my best to be more open about what I'd like to do, or what needs to be done, with the house and Peter."

"I believe you. I know you're an honest person, Christie. I didn't mean to imply that you were dishonest when you didn't tell me about the baby right away."

"I didn't take it that way."

He seemed genuinely relieved. "Good. Well then, would you like to go out, get away for a while? Not tonight, but when you…I mean, *we,* can get a babysitter?"

"A date?"

"That's what I was thinking. There's a movie theater in town with features on the weekends. Or…we danced pretty well together the other night, so we could go back to Dewey's. Or we could drive down to Graham to a restaurant there."

She was so surprised she couldn't think for a moment. Now that she'd moved in and had rejected the idea of getting married, he wanted to start dating? Besides, his request for a date seemed very practiced, as if he were an attorney making an argument.

Before she could respond, as her mouth was still open in surprise, her phone rang. She grabbed it, looking at the caller ID, thankful for even a momentary distraction. "Oh, it's local. Maybe it's Darla. I'd better answer this."

"Sure," Cal said before he turned and walked down the hallway, back toward his bedroom.

"I'm so glad you called, Darla," Christie said after the other woman had identified herself. Boy, was she glad. Cal had surprised her and she had to get herself together. "I'd like to talk to you if you're interested in caring for my son this summer. We'd need to meet, of course...."

CAL LET THE HOT WATER hit him full in the face as he stood beneath the shower. Although he'd practiced asking Christie out for a date after Burl had left, apparently he hadn't done a very good job since she hadn't given him an answer. Maybe she didn't want to pursue a relationship with him.

Her decision to move to Brody's Crossing might really be all about the baby. His need to get to know his son.

Which meant she really would be leaving, sooner rather than later.

He scrubbed a hand over his face, washing away the sweat and grime of the day, trying to clear his mind, as well. He didn't want Christie to leave, because then he'd never be sure if there was something between them, something as special as that weekend in Fort Worth.

And she'd take his son away before he ever got to know the boy. He'd never changed a diaper, fed him or done any of the other things fathers did now.

His own father hadn't participated in child rearing until he and Troy had been old enough for ranch chores. Then he'd been a good teacher and a strong father. That didn't mean his father's way of child rearing was the right way, especially in this day and age when women worked and men helped out around the house. He knew a lot more about men's roles since his reserve training and active duty. Mostly complaints, but some grudging acknowledgment that it took two to make a home.

So, he thought as he rinsed off the soap and shampoo, he had to find a better way to ask Christie out. Maybe if he hadn't been so grubby, he could have gotten closer to her, which might have been a step in the right direction…so to speak. He shook the water from his short hair, flinging drops over the tile. Maybe he should have waited to ask her until he got some flowers.…

He wasn't going to let this setback stop him, though. He wasn't going to throw up his hands in defeat. With more speed than usual, he went through the rest of his routine, shaving and dressing so he could get close to Christie if he could arrange the situation.

Which wasn't always easy with a baby between them.

By the time Cal finished, his stomach was growling. He hoped he had some beef in the freezer because he felt as if he could eat half a steer.

As he walked down the hallway, he heard Peter whimper. Cal stopped, his first instinct to go get Christie. But was that right? Surely he could handle comforting a baby. After all, he'd delivered more calves than he could count, had bottle-fed the orphans and doctored the ailing.

He stepped into the room, but even before he turned on a beside lamp, he knew something wasn't right.

That horrible odor couldn't come from a human infant.

Chapter Six

"I'm sorry," Cal said as they sat at the kitchen table, watching Peter play on the floor. "I had no idea what to do."

"It's okay," Christie said, reaching over and patting his arm. "Diapers and wipes and Diaper Genies can be confusing." Cal had tried to change Peter's diaper, but hadn't known how to handle a crying, squirming baby, an uncooperative diaper and a box of baby wipes that had failed to pop apart as promised. Plus, he hadn't known what to do with the messy diaper. "The important thing is that you tried."

"I honestly thought anyone could change a diaper."

"Well, sometimes it's tough. I hope this won't discourage you from trying again. Peter is normally great at diaper-changing time. However, watch out for the little water hydrant. He can soak you good if you're not careful."

Cal looked appalled at the prospect of getting sprayed by boy baby "plumbing," and she laughed at his expression. "You get used to all this. Remember that I've had nine months of 'active duty' with Peter while you were overseas. And I had a good baby-care class at the hospital before he was born. I knew very little about infants before that."

"I guess there was never a reason to learn."

Christie nodded and looked down at the table. "I would

sometimes even avoid my friends who had babies because it was too painful to be around all their happiness." The news that she couldn't have children had hit her hard.

"Did your…husband want to have children?"

"Honestly, it wasn't a big priority with him. We both thought there was plenty of time to explore our options. It wasn't until after Aldo's death that I realized I missed the idea of having a baby of my own, not particularly *his* child." That had been another blow because she'd thought they had been relatively happy. "I guess that means we weren't all that happy, but life seemed normal and fun at the time."

"I suppose you were living the good life."

"Yes, we were, but I see now that it was superficial. Restoring the old motel is giving me a lot more joy than shopping in Milan or lunching in Paris."

Cal looked skeptical.

"No, really, I'm enjoying this a lot."

"But what about running the motel once it's renovated? Will you enjoy taking reservations, checking in guests and getting all the rooms cleaned just as much?"

"Honestly, I'm not sure. If not, then I'll find someone to be the manager. I don't have to live on the property. I don't have to depend on the income to live, although I am hoping the motel will be self-sufficient in six months."

"You have a big investment in the property."

She shrugged. "Yes, but not as much as you might imagine. I got the motel for a song and I got many of the furnishings at thrift-store prices."

"That parking lot and the roof weren't cheap."

"No, but I can afford it. And really, it's exciting to see the motel come back to life."

"What if you decide to sell it?"

"I'm not planning to do that."

"But you could. You could leave town anytime."

"I could, but that's not what I want to do." At least, not now, as long as she and Cal were making progress in their relationship. "I'm building a new life here so Peter can grow up around both his parents."

Cal took a deep breath. "Okay."

"How about you? Did you want to get married and have children? Is my presence messing up any of your plans for someone in town?"

Cal snorted. "No! If I'd wanted to seriously date someone from town, I would have done so years ago. I'm thirty-six years old, and, yeah, I've thought about having a son."

"Not a child. A son."

"Well, yes, to carry on the ranching tradition and the name. Crawford men have sons and they ranch. I expected to carry on my name as soon as I got my military service out of the way."

Christie propped her head in her hands, elbows on the table. "So, who would you have married if you didn't have someone local in mind?"

Cal shrugged. "Maybe someone who'd moved to the area. Or a friend or family member of a local. A woman who enjoyed ranch life and was looking to raise a family." He looked her over in a way that made her want to squirm, then a slow, sexy grin spread across his tanned face. "Not a tall, built, blond social-ite who wouldn't normally give me the time of day."

"That's not true! I gave you more than the 'time of day,' if you recall."

"Oh, I recall just fine," he said, his voice low and intimate. "Do you ever think about that weekend?"

All the time. "Of course. Besides being the weekend we met, it's the weekend Peter was conceived. I think about that miracle every time I look at him."

Cal pulled back a little. "What about us? Do you ever wonder—"

The sound of crashing metal brought them both to their feet. Peter sat on the floor surrounded by several metal bowls that had rolled out of the cabinet door he'd managed to open.

"This is why we need baby locks," Christie said, walking across the floor and scooping him up. "He gets into so much stuff."

"I'll install whatever you want. As a matter of fact, why don't we go into town and see what they have at the hardware store."

"Right now?"

"No, it's too late now." He seemed to be deep in thought for a moment, then scowled. "Come to think of it, we shouldn't go into that hardware store at all. I'm sure they don't have anything you'd want."

Suddenly she understood. "Oh, you mean the hardware store that Toni's brother owns."

"Right. I'm sure it's way too small to satisfy your needs."

"You mean my baby-proofing needs?"

"All your needs. We should drive down to Graham tomorrow and shop there. They have a much bigger hardware store."

She smiled. "Oh, do they?"

"Yes, they do."

"Whatever happened to the small-town concept of 'shop local?'" she asked, shifting Peter to the other hip.

"Not always the best policy." Cal walked over until he was very close. He smelled like shampoo and soap, clean clothes and clean-cut male. "Would you show me how to handle the baby?"

The abrupt change in topic floored her, and for a few seconds, all she could do was stare. "Handle…as in pick up and hold?"

"That, and maybe how to change diapers."

"Gladly."

"And how do you know how much formula and water to put in those bottles? There are two different sizes. Why is that?"

Christie smiled. This she could do. Talking about Peter, showing Cal how to take care of his son. The topic was much safer than remembering how tall and muscular he looked in his plaid shirt and the clean, worn jeans that molded to his thighs. Much safer than breathing in his scent and thinking of burying her nose next to his neck. Maybe even licking his skin.

"Wow," she said, turning away. "Is it getting warm in here or is it just me? That air-conditioning is working okay, isn't it?"

"Why?" Cal asked, strolling to the counter. "Will you buy me a new one if it isn't?"

She stopped and watched him, but instead of the frown she expected, he actually smiled a little, as if he were teasing her. She smiled a little right back at him. "Maybe, but I'll only run it to the rooms Peter and I use."

Cal laughed then, and the mood lightened. She managed to get through an explanation of bottle preparation with the added bonus of passing Peter off to his father, who looked very natural holding him high against his chest.

"I wish I had my camera," she said softly as she watched father and son.

"This isn't the only time I'm planning on holding him."

"I know," she said, reaching out and straightening Peter's little Sesame Street T-shirt, "but it's the first day you've held him, and that's always special."

CHRISTIE HIRED DARLA JO Maxwell—she'd dropped her husband's last name now that she'd filed for divorce—the next day, after checking her references and criminal background. Darla seemed cheerful despite her recent separation.

And, most of all, Peter took to her almost magically. Darla had a natural way about her that appealed to children. Christie could understand why Darla was an excellent kindergarten teacher.

They arranged for Peter to be cared for from ten o'clock in the morning until four o'clock in the afternoon. That would give Christie time to get Peter up, play with him, feed him breakfast and get ready herself. Then she could go do her business and be back before supper. Darla was flexible, though, and said keeping Peter longer when Christie went to town on her buying trip wasn't a problem.

They toured the rooms that Christie used in the house—the bedroom she shared with Peter, their bath, the kitchen and living room—then strolled around the property in the hot afternoon sun to see the chickens, cows and, most of all, Riley. Peter loved the dog, who spent all his indoor time either under the baby's high chair, trying to snatch a falling goodie, or sleeping on the rug beside his bed.

"I'll see you on Monday, then," Darla said as they made their way back to her car. "I'm looking forward to working for you. I'd much rather be around a child than in a retail or service job for the summer."

"I understand," Christie replied. "I'm so glad you were available." She and Peter stood on the gravel drive and waved as Darla drove away.

Overjoyed, Christie wished she'd followed up on Cal's offer to go out to dinner or dancing or a movie. She felt as if she should celebrate. The decision to get help had been the right one. On impulse, she called Darla back on her cell phone and asked if she could babysit that night, in case Cal wanted to go out. They could go later than usual, though, to get Peter settled for the night first. Darla gladly agreed. The Maxwell property was very close, in terms of ranch distance, and Christie was sure the younger woman needed the money.

"Now," Christie said to Peter as they walked into the living room, "if I only had a date." She would simply ask Cal. She had no problem with a woman asking out a man, in principle, anyway. In practice, however, the task was sometimes difficult. What woman wanted to be shot down? What if the man was married, engaged or gay? Christie had misinterpreted a man's signals only once, but it wasn't an experience she wanted to repeat. Not that she was wrong about Cal, since he'd already asked *her*.

"Good grief," she said to Peter, sinking to the carpet beside him as he played with soft, bright-colored blocks. "I'm beginning to sound as if I'm in junior high school. Does he like me?" she sang, bobbing her head, making the baby laugh. "Will he go out with me?" She took Peter's chubby little hands and did a mock dance as they sat on the floor.

"Depends on who you're asking," Cal said, strolling into the room. "If you're talking about this cowboy, the answer is yes." With a flourish, he presented her with a bouquet of mixed flowers. "As a matter of fact, I was going to get back to you on that question I posed yesterday."

"Oh, thank you," she said, taking the flowers but holding them out of Peter's grasp, which made him reach up and fuss.

"I'll put these up for you if you'd like. I think I know where there's a vase. I didn't think about the baby wanting to play with them."

"They're colorful and they smell good, so of course he wants them. As a matter of fact, he'd rather eat them than play with them," Christie said with a big grin. "They're lovely."

Cal shrugged as he took back the bouquet. "We don't have a florist in town, so I couldn't get anything fancy. These are from the grocery store."

"Those are great. They match all of the colors that are now in the room."

Cal smiled. "Yeah, they do. So…what do you want to do tonight?"

"I just want to go out with a male who doesn't smell like baby lotion and doesn't wear a diaper."

"Well, that would be me. I may be a little older than you, but I'm not in Depends yet."

"You're terrible."

"I know, but I made you smile."

She felt her face almost hurt from so much unaccustomed grinning. "I know, and I like it."

Cal went into the kitchen, and Christie whispered to Peter, "I like it more all the time."

CAL VOLUNTEERED TO PLAY with the baby while Christie got fixed up for their date. The baby went from one toy to another, showing it to Cal and babbling, waving and grinning. He crawled like a pro and tried to pull himself up on everything in the room. "Baby-proofing" took on a whole new meaning from this angle. Cal suddenly saw that remotes, magazines and newspapers were fair game for the baby. At least he didn't have a bunch of knick-knacks lying around the place. Mostly, he supposed, they had to worry about what was in the cabinets the baby might open.

Cal found watching Peter fascinating. You could almost see the little wheels in his brain turning, trying to understand cause and effect, trying to see new ways he could use a toy. Mostly, Cal discovered, that involved throwing, hitting or stuffing it into something else. Still, this was his son, and he seemed as if he might be pretty smart and talented.

Darla arrived just as Peter was beginning to fuss and yawn. After Cal greeted her, she settled on the floor with Peter and began to play with him. He seemed a little suspicious at first, but was soon showing the babysitter his toys just as he'd presented them to Cal. Cal settled on the ottoman and watched them play.

Christie entered the room then, looking spectacular in a sleeveless, V-necked, coral dress that hit just above her knees. She looked really hot, from her tanned legs to her fluffed, curled hair.

"Darla, I thought maybe I'd have you watch our nightly routine and let Peter know that you're here. He usually goes to sleep pretty well, so as soon as he's down for the night, Cal and I can leave."

"Sounds good."

"I guess I'll watch some TV while you put him to bed, then," Cal said.

"Good idea. Tomorrow, you can do the nightly routine."

He knew his eyes widened at the idea of putting the baby to bed, but he'd asked to learn how to do things, so he didn't object. Instead, he grabbed a beer from the fancy new refrigerator, which held mostly fruits, vegetables, baby things, bottled water and diet soft drinks. What a change from his old fridge contents—beer, lunch meat, cheese and sometimes a bag of apples.

Christie and Darla walked into the room just as he was finishing his beer. "Ready?" Christie asked.

"More than ready. I could eat a horse."

"Uck. I hope not."

"Just kidding. Are we going to Dewey's?"

"That's fine with me." Christie turned to Darla. "You have my cell-phone number right, right?"

Darla reached into her pocket and held up her own phone. "Right here in my phone's memory. Don't worry. We'll be fine. Just have a good time."

As Cal escorted Christie outside, he thought about the differences in their vehicles. He had an old farm truck, while she drove a Cadillac. "Do you want to take your car or mine? Whatever you'd like is fine with me."

"Why don't you drive, if you don't mind."

"I don't mind. That's what I did in the military."

He opened the passenger door of the blue-and-faded-silver Ford 150. "Really? I don't think we ever talked about that."

He walked around to the driver's side and slid into the bench seat. "I drove an armored truck. Our convoys transported troops and supplies through the mountains and across streams from airfields to remote bases."

"Sounds dangerous."

He fingered the scar on his temple. "Sometimes."

After a moment, Christie said, "You know, for the first time, tonight I felt as if we were really parents. I got ready while you played with Peter. We got a babysitter, and now we're going out for dinner."

"So," Cal said, thinking through her remarks, "you felt more like we were parents than we were going out on a date."

"Well, yes. I suppose. It's hard to feel single when we're living in a house together and have a child. Although the flowers were very nice. Thank you again."

"You're welcome." He frowned as he turned out of the farm to Market Road. He'd wanted tonight to be a date. A real date. Now she felt as if they were a couple getting away from the baby for a night. This had ended up more about relief from routine than having fun with him.

"What's wrong?" Christie asked.

"Nothing. I'm just thinking."

"I'm sorry I mentioned Afghanistan. I didn't mean to bring up bad memories."

"What? You didn't."

"Oh."

Tell her, he scolded himself. *Explain what you're thinking.*

But he had a hard time making himself seem so…needy. "Nothing's wrong. I was just thinking about going out tonight. I hope you have a good time. I know you're used to more variety than one honky-tonk."

"Hey, it's a good honky-tonk. The food is great and the music last time was fun. I'm just glad we're going."

That relief thing again. "Yeah, me, too." Cal settled into the seat and told himself he didn't have to be too romantic since Christie was basically using their time together as a break from routine.

Inside, they walked through the restaurant portion toward a booth near the back. Cal greeted several neighbors, and to his surprise, Christie seemed to know quite a few people also. After they settled into the booth, he ordered a draft and Christie ordered a glass of white wine. That somehow made him feel better. Christie was a white wine kind of girl, and when she drank a beer or danced the two-step, she made it seem as if she was trying too hard to fit in.

If she was going to stay, then fine. But he'd believe it in about forty years or so. As far as he knew, she hadn't put her condo in Fort Worth on the market. Plus, she'd said she'd hire someone to run the motel if she didn't enjoy it. That didn't sound very permanent to him, even though she did claim to be building a new life here.

"So, tell me some more about your family. I know you and Troy don't always agree on things, but I'd like Peter to know more about his heritage."

"I can tell him when the time is right," Cal said, sounding a bit defensive. Hell, if she was going to stay around, why would *she* need to know *now?*

"What if something happened to you? He wouldn't know about his ancestors except on my side. I don't even know how to reach Troy and Raven."

"You know they're in New Hampshire."

"Yes, but although it's not nearly as big as Texas, I think it might be difficult to find two people among millions."

"I suppose," he said as a waitress he didn't recognize set their drinks before them. Cal told her they'd order in a few minutes, and she left.

"I'll write down Troy's new address and phone number for you at the house. It's no secret. I just didn't think about telling you."

"I'd appreciate that. And I'll leave you my attorney's name and phone number, along with other emergency information. Most of that I keep in my BlackBerry, if you ever need it. God, I hope you never need it!"

"James Brody—you met him and his wife Sandy at the going-away dinner the other night—mentioned that I should draw up a new will now that Peter has been born."

"I think that's a good idea."

"Before I left for active duty, I made a will leaving everything to Troy. That's all changed."

"I made a will also, just before my due date, leaving everything in trust for Peter in case there was a complication in the pregnancy. You never know about labor and delivery. Of course, I had to think mostly about his guardianship. I didn't want just anyone raising him."

"I'd raise him."

She gave him a look. "I didn't know you well then, and besides, you were out of the country. I hadn't told you about Peter, and I didn't know how you'd react."

"So, are you going to change your will now?"

"Yes, I intend to. My mother certainly doesn't want to raise another child."

Christie might have intentions, but she didn't say when, Cal observed. Did he have to pass a test to see if he was worthy of raising his son? Still, he didn't want to get angry at her for being cautious. He'd probably be the same way if their positions were reversed. "I'll talk to my attorney about drawing one up, too. If something happened to me, I'd want Peter recognized as my son and he'd eventually inherit my share of the ranch."

"That would be up to you, of course, but I think he'll appreciate that when he's older. And boy has this conversation gotten morbid! We're both young and nothing is going to happen to us for at least fifty years!"

"You never know," Cal said, taking a drink of his beer. "My father was fifty-two years old when he had an accident and died."

"Oh, that's terrible. Was it a car crash?"

"No, an accident with the tractor." A freak accident, the doctor had called it, but Doc didn't know all the details. He didn't know that Calvin Crawford had just told his oldest son that he wasn't worthy of running the Rocking C. "He was moving some round bales of hay when the lift broke." Cal shrugged away her sympathetic look. "There wasn't anything the paramedics could do."

"I'm so sorry. You were still young, then."

"Old enough." Despite his father's prediction, Cal had taken over running the Rocking C, and he'd done his old man proud, even if he was too late.

He motioned the waitress to their booth. "Are you ready to order?" he asked Christie as the waitress approached.

"Oh, I think I'll have a steak tonight."

"Good choice." He appreciated the fact that Christie wasn't a picky eater or, God forbid, a vegetarian like Raven.

They ordered, then talked about the four generations of Crawfords that had lived on the ranch. He remembered some interesting stories about his grandparents and great-grandparents that he'd forgotten until Christie asked.

After dinner, they enjoyed some dancing, but before long, the date part of the evening was over and Christie was back to being a concerned mother. Time to head back to the ranch.

"I HAD A REALLY GOOD TIME," Christie said as they rolled to a stop near the back door of the house. The outdoor mercury vapor security lights were on. Riley was inside the house with Darla and Peter, so they weren't greeted with barking.

Cal turned off the engine, then rolled down his window. The warm, fragrant night air drifted through the dark cab of the truck. "Me, too."

"It was good to see some of your neighbors."

"Your neighbors now, too."

"You're right. I'm still getting used to being a member of the community."

"How long, Christie?"

She turned to face him more fully. "How long what?"

"How long do you think you'll be here? I've heard you say the motel renovations are going well, and I'm getting to know my son. But what about you? How long can you stand living in a town without a Barnes & Noble or a Starbucks, not to mention a spa or a major department store?"

"You think I'm that superficial?"

"No, but I think the reality of living here will hit you sooner or later. You're a city girl at heart."

"I made the decision to move here and buy property," she said, getting angry that he thought she was acting on a whim. "And besides, you hardly know me well enough to tell me what I am or am not."

"I guess you're right about that, about not knowing you. I'm trying to, though. That's why I thought we should date, since we never did that before."

"You say you're trying to know me, but I'm not sure that's

true. Don't you have too many preconceived notions about me to keep an open mind?"

"I didn't say I was perfect."

"No, but you said you were trying. Are you?"

He leaned closer, his eyes flickering with the mercury lights. "I'll tell you what I am. I'm frustrated because I'm not sure what to do next. All night I've wondered whether you really wanted to be on a date with me, or you just wanted to get out for a while. You're right that I don't know you, but I remember you. I remember every damn thing about you from a year and a half ago. I remember the feel of your skin and the smell of your hair, how you hang up your towels and what side you sleep on. I remember that you love English muffins and can't stand bagels."

Her breath shallow and fast, she whispered, "You remember all that?"

"Yes," he said, cupping her jaw. "And more." And then he kissed her.

Chapter Seven

Christie was so surprised by Cal's kiss that she sat perfectly still, her lips parted, for just a second or so. Then the sensation of being in his arms rushed through her, and her instincts took over.

She leaned into his hard chest while he slanted his mouth over hers, as the kiss went on and on. She felt as if she might pass out from lack of oxygen but she didn't care.

When he broke the kiss, breathing heavily, she was lying on the vinyl upholstery, his hands shoved into her hair. She welcomed his weight, crushing her into the bench seat. It had been so long. So long…

"I remembered right," he whispered against her neck, sending goose bumps down her bare arms and legs.

"What?" Her brain wasn't working. How could she think when he was kissing that spot below her ear?

"We should get up," he said, his voice low and seductive.

She shifted and came fully against his arousal. More goose bumps. More breathlessness.

"We should go into the house," he said. "I'm willing to continue this in your bedroom or mine, but maybe we should—"

"No, you're right. We should get into the house," Christie said, snapping out of her sensual coma. "Darla probably heard the truck and will wonder what we're doing out here."

"In that case," Cal said, "I'd better fix your hair." He ran his fingers through the strands, smoothing it back in place.

"Um, thanks," Christie said as she opened the truck door and jumped out. She hadn't made out in a front seat—or a back seat, for that matter—in more years than she cared to consider. When Cal had kissed her, though, her mind had stopped working. She hadn't thought of where she was or how she might look afterward. She rubbed beneath her eyes in case her mascara had smeared, then straightened her clothes. Cal walked around to her side.

"Ready?"

She nodded. He put his arm around her shoulders as they walked toward the back door. "Cal?"

"Yes?"

"I don't think I'm ready to continue…beyond what just happened," she said, waving toward the truck. She took a deep breath. "I'm not sure I'm ready to take our relationship to the next level. Well, not yet."

"I didn't really expect you to spend the night in my bed. Or me in yours. Not tonight."

"What if I'd said I was ready?" she asked, halting at the back steps.

"I would have considered myself the luckiest man in the world."

She thought about his honesty for a moment, then asked, "Are you saying you don't expect a girl to put out on a first date?"

His grin lit up the night. "That's what I'm saying." He pulled her close and kissed her again, this time briefly. He didn't give her time to melt. "Now, watch out on that second date, though." He dropped his arms and stepped around her.

"I'll keep that in mind," she said softly as he unlocked the back door.

ON SUNDAY AFTERNOON, Cal, Christie and Peter attended a little welcome-home reception in his honor at the Crawford-Peet VFW Post, just outside of town. Cal hadn't wanted to bring the baby because of the smoking, but he'd been promised that due to the mild weather, they'd have it outdoors on the patio.

"The post is named after your family?" Christie asked as she followed his directions toward Olney. The day was sunny and the pastures were still green from springtime rain.

"Partially. My grandfather was decorated in World War II. Before that, it was the Peet VFW Post. He was a World War I soldier from the area."

"So military service is part of your family tradition?"

"Yes, U.S. Army, but only for the guys."

"I'm not sure how I'd feel about Peter carrying on that tradition."

"I had to put off serving because Troy went to college, then moved away, and I had the ranch. Finally, I felt I had the right solution, and I joined the reserves in the summer of 2001. I would spend only one weekend a month and two weeks in the summer, and Troy volunteered to take his vacation during my annual duty. My next six years were planned out—and then 9/11 happened."

She was quiet for a moment, then asked, "Did you know right away that you'd be called up?"

Cal shrugged. "When we went into Afghanistan, I wasn't sure. But then Iraq…and I pretty much figured I'd be activated." The idea of leaving the ranch, maybe even losing it, had frightened him. At night, alone in the office his father had used before there were computers, he'd wondered how he could run the place when he was halfway around the world. Troy wasn't a rancher any longer. Like all ranchers, Cal was into the bank for operating expenses until he sent the beeves to the feed lot. One of the things he loved about the ranch was the cycle of the seasons.

One of the things that got old was the incredible amount of hard, physical labor at certain times of the year. Calving, dosing, castrating, inoculating. Big ranches had more hands, more automation, more conveniences. He had his own two hands and two cowboys to help on a regular basis.

"How do you feel about Peter ranching someday?" he asked.

"I'm...I'm getting used to the idea that it might be an option."

"What do you mean, an option?"

"What if he doesn't like to ranch?"

He stared at her, then turned back to look at the sleeping baby. "He's a Crawford. He'll like to ranch."

"I don't know, Cal. I'm not comfortable forcing him into a profession that doesn't fit his personality or abilities."

"He'll learn to appreciate the tradition."

"What if he's a brilliant concert pianist, or a talented baseball player or wants to be a doctor? How can you say that he *must* ranch if he has different goals?"

Cal felt his face tighten and his stomach clench. He had a son, but no right to guide his development. The helplessness of the situation made him feel as if he should shout, make himself understood. The date with Christie had gone pretty well, especially there at the end after a disappointing start, but he didn't feel any closer to getting married. She could still leave anytime and take the baby with her. James Brody had told him that just because Cal was named the father on the birth certificate, it wouldn't make it any easier to get custody away from Christie.

"We have a few years before he chooses his profession," Cal said, tamping down his frustration...again. "Right ahead is the VFW post. Just pull in anywhere on the side."

He hadn't wanted to come to this shindig, but now he was

grateful he didn't have to talk to Christie about his son's future anymore. They obviously had as many differences when it came to child rearing as they did in the rest of their lives.

Christie was a great mother, but she had different opinions and different values than a small-town rancher. She didn't understand. Because she was wealthy, she could change her life on a whim.

She could leave simply because she wanted to. He couldn't trust her to stay just because she said she *intended* to do so. There was nothing to tie her to him or the ranch. She wouldn't even consider getting married.

Of course, marriage hadn't stopped his mother from leaving her family. If he couldn't trust his own mother to stay, how could he trust Christie?

"It worries me that Cal is so set on making Peter into a rancher," Christie told Bobbi Jean Maxwell a little later that afternoon, as the men shared a beer inside and the women enjoyed cake on the patio. "Cal is so set on tradition."

"That's the way of a lot of men are around here. It's first nature to most ranchers. There's no sense building up a ranch if you think you're going to walk away. It's not like a job you retire from."

"Cal mentioned his father died at such a young age. Did you know him well?"

"As well as anyone knew Calvin Crawford. He was even more of a loner than Cal. At least Cal likes to socialize occasionally. I don't think you could pry Calvin away from the Rocking C unless you had a pretty big crowbar, and believe me, after a while, it wasn't worth the work."

"I hadn't realized he was almost reclusive."

"Cal's father worked harder than two men combined, but if you ask me, most of that work was spent on keeping things the way they were. Or the way he thought they should be. It about killed him to build that house when he and Luanna got married because he'd wanted to fix the old one. Repair the foundation, update the walls and floor for his bride, that sort of thing. But the old house wasn't fixable, and had to be torn down."

"I can see that. Cal's a bit defensive about the house, too. I bought a few new appliances since Peter and I moved in. I thought Cal would be pleased, but instead, it seemed as if I was taking over. We've gotten past it, though."

"Most men around here, ranchers, are proud. They want to make the money and provide for their wives and children."

"I like taking care of myself. Maybe that's why I wouldn't make a good wife. Cal must see that."

"Men see what they want to see. You're the mother of his child. In his mind, that means you should also be his wife."

Christie sighed. "He won't even call Peter by his name anymore. Cal calls him 'the baby' or 'my son.' I know he was upset that I didn't name him Calvin Peter Crawford V, but how was I to know that meant so much? I did my best at the time, waiting to tell Cal in person. It's like he's angry at me for that decision, and that hurts, Bobbi Jean."

She patted Christie's hand. "Of course it does. Have you talked to him about your feelings?"

"Not yet. We haven't had time. There are so many other things to talk about. And we went on a 'date' last night, so I didn't want to hit him with criticism then."

"Good thinking. Maybe you could make him a nice meal. Men are more amenable with a full stomach."

"That's a good idea. I haven't had time to cook a real meal yet. All I've done is warm things up and make sandwiches."

"Cal should have some beef in the freezer, or ask him to stop by the grocery on the way home for some chicken or pork. That's something the two of you can do together."

"There are so many things we *haven't* done together."

Bobbi Jean laughed, surprising Christie. "Hon, that's probably true, but the evidence of at least one of the things you two did together is about to pull your cake into his lap."

Christie grabbed the paper plate just in time to avert a mess. "Thanks for the heads-up. I guess this *one thing* is pretty obvious." She handed Peter his sippy cup so he wouldn't miss the cake as much. "I'm just not sure if it's enough to base a relationship on."

Bobbi Jean patted her hand again. "Only time will tell. You and Cal both seem like hard workers. Just remember to save a little of your energy for your private moments."

Clarissa, Ida and a few other women brought their own cake and drinks over to visit and admire Peter. Christie could almost imagine that this is what family should feel like, as if these were all Peter's great-aunts. Soon, with all the chatter, Christie didn't have time to think about Cal much at all, much less those "private moments" Bobbi Jean had mentioned.

As a matter of fact, she spent a lot of energy trying not to think about the private moments in the truck last night. Giving in to temptation would complicate matters tremendously, especially when she knew Cal was looking forward to wedding cake rather than welcome-home cake, and shared custody of Peter rather than a shared living room at the house.

No, she'd better watch herself around Cal Crawford. His kisses were trouble with a capital *T.*

"THE PARTY WAS VERY NICE," Christie said as she placed a platter of chicken and pasta on the kitchen table.

"Yeah, it was nice of them to do that. A lot of trouble for everyone, though."

"I think they enjoyed getting together. I know I had a good time with Bobbi Jean, Ida and Clarissa. Peter took to them, also."

The baby sat in his high chair, making a mess of some of the pasta and sauce. He looked as if he was finger-painting. Then he picked up a handful of green beans and stuffed them in his mouth. "He's not going to choke, is he?" Cal asked Christie.

"No, he has some teeth, and he does chew. Mostly he gums his vegetables into submission."

"Looks messy."

"My mother would have a fit over his 'abominable' table manners, but he's just a baby. He doesn't need to know how to use a spoon and fork yet."

"You're the expert."

Cal took a bite of the pasta and was surprised at how good it tasted. "So, your mother wasn't all that supportive about the baby?"

"Not really. I don't think she has a grandmotherly bone in her body. And since Peter was born out of wedlock, he's a bit of an embarrassment to her among her highbrow friends."

"It's a good thing I don't know your mother," Cal said, taking a sip of the iced tea Christie had made. "I don't think I could put up with her saying anything bad about Peter's birth."

"She wouldn't…well, she *probably* wouldn't say anything directly to you. She's very good about talking around an issue. She's passive-aggressive."

"Well, if she bad-mouths you or the baby, I'm just going to be aggressive." He looked up to see Christie trying to hide a grin.

"What's so funny?"

"You're so adamant about defending us."

"It's not your fault. Well, it's kind of *our* fault, but I don't think it should reflect on a child."

Christie reached for the platter and dished some food out

onto her plate. "I absolutely agree. How about around here? What do they think about our situation?"

Cal shrugged. "Most of them probably think we should get married. But then, I'm not really worried about other people."

"Then why do you want to get married? That is, if you still do."

"Because I think it's the right thing to do for the baby and for us, since we're living in the same house."

"But if other people aren't criticizing us, then why—"

"Doing what's right isn't about getting criticized. It's about knowing it deep inside. My father taught me that, and I expect to teach…Peter someday."

"You called him Peter!"

"Yeah, well, that's still tough for me."

"If he were named Calvin Peter Crawford, what would you call him?"

"What do you mean?"

"Well, your father was Calvin, and you're Cal. What would Peter be?"

"Hell, I don't know!"

"Well, think about it. Would he be 'Little Cal,' or 'C.P.' or what?"

Cal narrowed his eyes and frowned at her, but she didn't seem intimidated. Damn. That had usually worked in the army with his eighteen-year-old privates when their sergeant wasn't happy with them.

"I'm going to the motel tomorrow, as soon as Darla gets here. Would you like to come with me?"

"Why?"

"I thought you might like to see it. I mean, you probably remember when it was still open, right?"

"I guess so. It was a dump then. No one wanted to stay there."

"It's going to be fantastic when I'm finished."

"It's going to be damned expensive."

"I know, but I'm in it for the long haul," Christie said, completely oblivious to the realities of life. Few people could be that unconcerned about how much something cost and how much revenue they'd have coming in. Cal wanted to shake his head at her approach to the renovation.

"I might want to see it, but maybe not tomorrow."

"I'm taking photos and measurements tomorrow. I could use some help."

Cal toyed with his food, tempted beyond his better sense. "I guess I can go after I get the morning chores done." Not that he had a lot to do. Bison were pretty hands-off except for parasite control and vaccinations in the fall. He fed the horses and the laying hens and worked on maintenance of the fences and property.

"What time?"

"Around nine o'clock."

"I'll be ready about ten, when Darla gets here," Christie said. "I want to make sure she's settled in with Peter before I leave. She's working ten until four, by the way."

"Okay then." He ate a few more bites of pasta and picked at his green beans. "Dinner is really delicious, by the way."

"Thanks," Christie said with a smile. "I have it on a good authority that men are more agreeable on a full stomach."

"That's not the only way."

"I know, but chicken and pasta is all you're getting tonight."

Cal chuckled and finished his meal. Living with a woman was a strange and stimulating experience, one he'd never tried before. He could get used to Christie, though.

If she stayed.

CHRISTIE FELT a little guilty about asking Cal to come with her to the motel, she thought as she inserted a small hoop into her ear. She didn't absolutely need him or his opinion. As a matter of fact, he'd made his views on renovating the hotel very clear. He thought her idea of reopening the Sweet Dreams was absurd. She thought he was narrow-minded. Just one more way that they disagreed.

She pulled on her athletic shoes and straightened her socks. There was no sense wearing flimsy shoes when she'd be walking through what was sure to be a mess. It might be a demolition zone at the moment, but soon it would be fabulous.

With or without Cal's support.

Still, it was nice that he'd agreed to join her. She'd asked him because of Raven's request to keep him busy so he wouldn't try to change the ranch back to the way it was before. If Cal had asked her opinion, she would have told him emphatically that the diversity of the animals seemed like such a good idea. Besides, she loved to drive under the Rocking C arch, up to the house, with pastures filled with bison, cows, chickens and cattle.

She loaded up her tote bag and purse, then met Cal in the kitchen. He was having one last cup of coffee. He'd also showered after his morning chores, so he smelled really good.

"Do you think we should sneak out, or tell Peter goodbye?" she asked. Darla was in the living room, deep in baby play with the large blocks Peter loved.

"I vote for slipping out. There's no need to upset him."

Christie nodded. They quietly opened the back door, then Cal locked it once they were out. "We should get Darla a key made while we're out."

"Good idea. I don't have any extras."

Christie drove in companionable silence toward town. They passed the church on one side, and the feed store and garage on the other just down the block. At Main Street, she turned left and continued down another two blocks, just out of the downtown area. The old motel sat by itself, surrounded by empty lots. Lonely concrete foundations showed that these places had once been occupied by homes or businesses. Some of them were badly crumbled. A few bushes and flowers pushed up through the rocks and soil, giving more evidence that people had once lived and worked there.

Hopefully, with the opening of the motel and the few other businesses that had been established last year, such as the farmers' market and the butcher shop, Brody's Crossing would grow out toward the Sweet Dreams.

"This area is a dump," Cal said, shattering her idyllic vision of the future.

"Well, I'll bet it wasn't always that way, and with a lot of work, it can be nice again."

"Don't tell me you're going to buy up the whole block and build on these empty lots!"

"I hadn't planned on it, but thanks for the idea."

Christie would have bet Cal was rolling his eyes as she pulled into the parking lot, next to Toni Casale's big extended-cab pickup. "Looks like Toni has her full crew working this morning." Christie was paying extra to ensure the construction crew wasn't split between multiple jobs so she could get the motel open in time for Labor Day weekend.

All the doors were off the units. A big metal trash container was full of wood, carpet, linoleum and old cabinets.

"Hi, Christie. Cal," Toni called out from near the office.

They detoured to the asymmetrical, aluminum-and-glass-framed office. Some of the original stickers from the 1960s remained on the extremely dirty windows. MasterCard, Diners Club, Best Western and a few logos that Christie didn't recognize had faded in the Texas sun.

"How's it going?" she asked her contractor.

"Well, we came across some problems in the office. Come on in and I'll show you."

Cal followed them into the hot, dusty office, where Toni pointed out a crack running diagonally across the concrete slab. "We pulled out the old carpet and linoleum underneath and found some structural issues. This is pretty severe. Normally, I'd advise you to rip it out and repour a new slab."

"But would we be able to save the original aluminum-framed windows?"

"I'm not sure. We wouldn't know until we started the demo."

"Oh." This was really disappointing. She loved the 1950s style of the office.

"We might be able to get close to the original design, but those angles are going to be expensive to engineer."

"I really wanted to keep the original structure."

"Another option would be having a foundation expert come out. We may need to add some concrete work to the outside to build up the slope down to the parking lot, which has deteriorated over the years. We'd also have to disassemble some of the front, but I'm pretty sure we can do that with a minimum of damage, even to the glass."

"Good. Let's do that, as long as it doesn't put us too far behind schedule."

"Okay, then. I'll get him out here ASAP."

"Whatever you need to do." Christie looked around. "I also want to save the original check-in desk and the slots for keys and mail. Could you make sure they're marked?"

"Absolutely."

"I'm going to show Cal around and take some measurements."

"Come and see me before you leave," Toni said. "I have the linoleum samples for you."

"Great! See you in a few."

They'd barely walked out of earshot when Cal asked, "Do you have any idea how much people can take advantage of you when you give them a blank check?"

"Yes, I think I have an idea. I wasn't born yesterday."

"Yeah, but you're throwing good money after bad! This place is a shell. Rebuilding it will cost more than tearing the damn thing down and building a new, modern motel."

"I know that. I knew that going in."

"Then why are you so intent on wasting your money on this remodeling nightmare?"

"Because I want *this* motel, not a new one. Because I see it as an opportunity, not a disaster. I see the potential, not just the problems. I'm trying to be realistic, Cal, but honestly, it's all part of a plan."

"A plan? More like a day-to-day money pit."

"Well, it's my money pit, and I think it's going great."

"How can you say that?"

"I guess I'm just an optimist." She walked through the doorway of the unit on the far end. This was the largest room since it was on a corner, and it had an extra picture window on the side.

"This is going to be the honeymoon suite," she told Cal, who still looked ready to argue with her. "I'm putting a nice seating area in here, plus a Jacuzzi tub in the bathroom. I need to see if a king-size bed and a couple of chairs will fit." She pulled her tape measure out of her tote bag.

"Do you think people will drive all the way to Brody's Crossing for their honeymoon?"

She handed Cal the end of the tape and walked across the room. "I absolutely believe they'll come here to stay at a restored vintage motel with modern conveniences. Maybe not for a honeymoon, unless they're into kitsch, but how about an anniversary? Or just a special weekend? I think it will be romantic. Please go to the opposite wall."

He looked around the space. "I guess you can see things I can't, because it looks like a mess to me."

She wrote down the measurement on her notepad. "The only thing I'm debating is whether to keep any of the original knotty pine paneling. It's vintage and original to the structure, but too much of it makes the place look like a cabin rather than a retro hotel." She gestured toward the other wall. "Could you stand over there, please?"

He walked to the outside wall. "We went on a trip to my mother's family reunion in Arkansas once. We stayed in one of those tourist courts, you know the ones with the separate cabins? That place had the knotty pine paneling all the way to the ceiling. It was kind of cool when I was a kid, but I can see where too much of it would be overwhelming. Maybe you could just keep it in a room or two."

"You mean not have all the rooms the same?" She wrote down the other measurement, then looked up at Cal.

He shrugged. "Why not? You might get women or men, or couples or families. You could have different rooms for different tastes."

She walked to the doorway of the honeymoon suite and looked back down the overhang, all the way to the office. Thirteen units. She would renovate ten into individual rooms, combine two for an owner's suite, and use the one next to the office for a lounge-slash-conference center, complete with modern amenities such as wireless Internet, a tiki bar and a flat-panel TV.

She'd envisioned ten identical retro rooms, but now, as she looked, she could see different-colored doors on the units. Names in the brochure. Subtle themes, perhaps, or not real names, but varying decors. Blond wood with tapered legs, dark walnut Danish modern, bright molded plastic and bright chrome. Gone was the pressure to find ten identical head-boards, dressers, artwork…

Christie turned back to Cal, walked over and framed his face with her hands. "You're a genius," she said before giving him a smacking kiss on the lips.

Chapter Eight

"What?" he stammered when Christie abruptly pulled back. He hadn't reacted fast enough to grab her and hold on. Now she was practically skipping across the floor, as excited as a chicken with a june bug.

"Your idea to make each room different. I'm going to do it! That solves all my problems of finding identical retro furniture or buying expensive reproductions to match."

"Okay," he said cautiously. He hadn't considered his idea such a brilliant suggestion. Just a common sense assumption.

"I was thinking along the lines of a Simmons Hotel Group property. We make all the rooms match for a particular hotel in specific room types. For example, a suite will have a table and two chairs, and perhaps an extra easy chair in addition to the bed and nightstands. But this is the best idea. I can shop for individual items that will make the rooms unique. People will love that. After all, if I'm appealing to boomers and retro-addicts, they all have their own memories of their childhood home, or their own preferences."

Cal shrugged. "I'm glad I could help, but I still think the whole thing is a waste of time and money."

"Yes, yes, I know how you feel. Get over it, okay? I'm

doing this and now I'm even more excited than before. I can't wait to go shopping!"

Get over it? No one had told him that in years.

He and Christie finished the measurements for the other nine rooms, which they found had identical dimensions. Only the "honeymoon suite" and the three gutted suites near the office were different.

"I'm starving," Christie said as she placed her items back in her tote bag. "Let's see Toni, then go to lunch. Oh, and we need to have that key made."

Making a key, he'd realized sometime after the suggestion had been made and seconded, meant going to the hardware store. The one owned by that blond Adonis who loved to flirt with Christie. "Maybe we should get back and check on the ba…Peter."

Christie glanced at her watch. "He's probably having lunch right now, then he'll go down for a nap. I'll text-message Darla and see how he's doing. That way, if he's sleeping, it won't wake him." She whipped out her BlackBerry and created a message faster than he could dial a regular telephone.

They found Toni in the office, on her cell phone. She finished, then placed the various tiles on the floor. Soon, Christie picked two colors she liked. They had to be ordered from a warehouse in Dallas, but the repairs to the slab had to come first.

"So, in the rooms, do you want wood, laminate or these tiles?" Toni asked.

"Cal had a brilliant idea. I'm making each room different. That way, I can buy whatever furniture I find and pick the flooring based on the colors."

"You might want to go with a neutral," Toni advised, "in case the furniture changes in the future. We could put in a laminate that would blend with almost any color or style."

"Let me think about that. The idea is still formulating."

"Okay, just let me know in about ten days or so. We'll start prep work on the floors then. Of course, we still have a lot of drywall and cabinet installation to go."

"I won't delay the schedule," Christie promised.

Soon they were finished at the motel and headed back down Main Street. Cal looked back once, trying to see the old place as Christie did. Maybe there was something worth salvaging there. Maybe it would be nice when she was finished.

But it was still a lot of money spent on an old-fashioned project with little hope of a profit.

He frowned as he recalled several rancher friends and even his brother telling him the same thing about raising Herefords. *That's the past,* they claimed. *You have to modernize,* they advised.

But dammit, the old ways had worked for over a hundred years. Why did *he* have to be the one who changed course? Why couldn't he *make* it work? The other Crawford men had kept the ranch going, maybe not strong, but at least afloat.

"Is the café okay?" Christie asked.

"Sure." Although the place was sure to be full of chatty women and retired men at this time of the day. Oh, well. He'd gotten used to them being in his business ever since he'd come back from Afghanistan. He, Christie and the baby—Peter—were the current hot topic, and probably would be until the next big event came along.

He just hoped something else happened soon so he wouldn't generate so much gossip and speculation. What Brody's Crossing needed was a new scandal.

Cal ate his chopped steak plate lunch as fast as he could and still maintain table manners. "I'll go get that key made while you finish up," he offered.

"What's the hurry? I can finish and go with you."

"I, er, need to get back to the ranch."

"But what if I need something else at the hardware store? I like to look around. Hardware stores are fascinating."

"Not this one," Cal muttered.

"What?"

"Nothing. I just think I can get the key made much more quickly if I'm by myself."

Understanding seemed to dawn. "You don't want me around Leo Casale, do you?"

"He's way too friendly. Have a piece of pie. I'll be back soon." Cal skedaddled out of the café as fast as possible, Christie's chuckles echoing in his head.

LATER THAT NIGHT, Christie stayed up long after Peter had gone to sleep. The house was so quiet. Even Riley had retired for the night, sleeping on a braided rug next to Peter's crib. Christie's long-held desire for a yellow Lab had completely disappeared now that Riley and Peter had bonded. A little boy couldn't have a better dog than the "mutt" Raven had found beside the road.

The vintage magazines Christie used for inspiration lay open on the coffee table, tabbed with sticky notes. She should probably create a portfolio of color copies before going on her buying trip later in the week. Also, she needed to look at flooring choices to decide whether she'd go with one material for all the rooms or several, to give more variety.

"Are you still up?" a soft, sleepy voice said from the hallway.

Her heart sped up a little when she heard Cal's voice, then she looked at him in the shadows of the hallway. He wore boxers and nothing else. Her heart rate picked up to double-time. "I was too excited to sleep."

"I was going to get a glass of milk."

"Couldn't you sleep, either?"

"I had a little heartburn."

"Mmm-hmm." He'd declared her red beans and rice were

too mild and had proceeded to add a generous amount of hot sauce to his plate. They'd fixed corn bread from a mix and he'd shared his secret ingredient—a spoon of sugar in addition to the egg and milk. It was tasty. Peter had really liked corn bread with his green beans and mandarin orange slices.

"Yeah, you can say 'I told you so' if you want."

"I didn't try to tell you anything," she corrected him. She had, however, given him a look that said "What the heck are you doing?"

"Do you want anything?" he asked as he stepped into the kitchen.

Yes. I want you to put on some clothes. "No, I'm fine," she said, turning her attention back to her magazines. She wasn't about to show him how much the sight of his body affected her. He seemed more muscular than she remembered. Maybe he'd lifted weights while in the military. Maybe her memory wasn't so good.

"What are you studying?"

"What?" Her head shot up. She had no idea what she'd been studying. All she could see was Cal's chest and arms and shoulders, and boy, was she in trouble. "Oh, just some magazines from 1962 to 1964 that I found at Half-Price Books. I'm getting ideas." Boy, was she getting ideas, and few of them had anything to do with decorating her motel.

"My grandparents had some stuff that looked like that," Cal said, placing his glass of milk on the coffee table and sitting down on the couch beside Christie. The soft cushions immediately leaned toward his greater weight, and she fought to stay upright and in control of her senses.

"I wish I had their furniture now. It would make my life easier. I wouldn't have to do so much shopping."

"I think they got rid of everything. We could look in the

attic, though. There might be some stuff left up there. If so, you'd be welcome to it."

"Oh, I couldn't take your family furniture for the motel."

Cal shrugged, then took a sip of milk. He had a faint milk mustache that she really wanted to taste. "Whatever. I'd rather somebody get some use out of the old stuff, if any of it is still around."

"What do you think they did with their furniture when they got rid of it? Would they have trashed it, given it away or sold it?"

"They probably gave it to someone who had less than they did. I'm not sure who, but I remember a couple of families they knew through the church. You could ask Ida Bell. She'd probably know because she and my mother were friends way back then."

"I'll do that. If I could track any of it down, it would give a great history to the motel."

"I'm sure the furniture is in pretty poor condition."

"It can be fixed."

He put the empty glass on the table. "Can it?"

She drew in a deep breath. "Almost anything can be fixed."

"How about us? What's the diagnosis for our relationship?"

"I…I'm not sure yet."

He twirled a strand of her hair around his finger. "I guess I came on a little too strong again today. About the motel, I mean. I'm not used to having money to spend like that. You've got to know that I watch every penny."

"I know you do. I appreciate that, but I'm not in the same situation. I see the motel as a long-term investment."

"Investment, but not necessarily a job."

"I don't have to work. Besides, being a mother is the best job ever." Hadn't they already talked this over? He obviously didn't believe her. He didn't trust her to stay. "I might have bought the Sweet Dreams on a whim, but I didn't move to Brody's Crossing without giving it serious thought."

His fingers moved to her temple and she closed her eyes. "Well, that's good," he said, his breath tickling her skin. She parted her lips, and then he kissed her.

This time they weren't in the front seat of a pickup truck and no babysitter was waiting inside for them. This time Christie knew there was no physical or situational reason why she couldn't relax and enjoy herself…and him.

He tasted like milk and warm, sleepy male. He smelled like clean shampoo and soap and *man,* all wrapped up in tousled sheets. The kiss pushed her into the back cushions and she instinctively put up her hand to hold him away, just a little, until she could get her bearings.

But the minute she touched his warm, tight, bare shoulder, she was a goner. He felt really good. Too good to resist. She slanted her head and matched his tongue, thrust for thrust, and sucked his bottom lip when they both broke for air.

"Does going to the motel and then lunch today count as a second date?" he whispered against her lips.

"What?" Her head was spinning and he wanted to talk logistics? "Why are we counting?"

"Because I don't want to rush you, but I really want to make love to you. With you. Again."

Ah, this was Cal. The man who thought there was a right way and a wrong way to do everything. Even make love. Or decide when to make love. She recalled that he'd been very open to actually making love in a wide variety of ways and places, with no thought of whether they were on a first date or a third. That was on her turf. Now they were on his, and he had something in mind. Something more than making each other feel good.

"I'm not going to make love on a schedule," she said, pulling herself back from the brink of a sensual abyss.

"No schedule," he murmured against her neck.

Goose bumps raced down her spine. "I need to go to bed."

"Excellent idea. I'll go with you," Cal offered.

"No," she said, hoping she sounded more certain than she felt. "Not now. Not tonight."

"Why?"

"Because there's too much unresolved between us."

"This might be a good opportunity to resolve some of those issues," he said, no longer kissing her skin but still holding her tightly against his hard body and the soft couch.

"I don't think making love will resolve anything. I think it will just make our lives more complicated and confusing."

Cal moaned against her shoulder. "You think too much, Christie."

She pushed and he levered himself away. She scooted off the couch, her shorts and top badly crumpled and her emotions in a jumble. "Someone has to think for both of us," she said as she flipped her hair out of her eyes. "I'm going to bed—alone. I'll see you in the morning."

Cal closed his eyes, collapsed against the cushion and groaned again. As she fled down the hall, she glanced back at the couch just once, seeing a very frustrated man with washboard abs, far from innocent boxers covering his goods, sprawled where she'd been happily poring over vintage mags just minutes before.

This is in your own best interest, she told herself as she closed the door on her bedroom. Still, despite knowing what was the logical and practical decision, she found resisting Cal was becoming more and more difficult. Good thing she was leaving soon for a few days of sanity.

WITHOUT CHRISTIE AND PETER in the house, the place echoed with Cal's solitary footsteps and Riley's sad whining. Christie had even taken Darla with her to watch the baby, and they were staying at the condo in Fort Worth. They'd been gone for only a day, and already Cal felt the loss.

What if they'd left for good?

He'd lived alone in this house for most of his adult life, yet only now did he feel lonely. Upon returning from Afghanistan, he'd thought that the sounds of silence and the routine of chores would soothe him after the stress of living in a war zone. And maybe they would have, if he'd experienced any of the silence and routine. Ever since he'd returned, he'd been around family and neighbors and now, Christie and the baby.

Peter. He did have a hard time thinking of the boy by that name. Peter Simmons Crawford. Sounded preppy. Not nearly as substantial as Calvin Peter Crawford V. Maybe he could talk her into changing the baby's name. They could still call him Peter. He'd give in to that. Compromise was the name of the game, right?

He hadn't argued with Christie the night before last, when she'd kissed him like she never wanted to stop, then jumped up and ran for her bedroom. He hadn't meant to kiss her or anything else when he'd gotten up for a glass of milk. He'd assumed she was in bed and had perhaps forgotten to turn off the light when he'd made his way down the hallway. If he'd known she was up, he would have pulled on some jeans. Probably. The way she'd looked at his body was enough to turn him on now if he let himself remember.

Late in the morning, he opened the fold-down stairs to the attic. He'd promised Christie anything that might be up there from the 1960s. He hooked a flashlight in his waistband and ascended the dusty stairs.

After looking around for ten minutes or so in the hot attic, he found only a few things she might be interested in. A couple of lamps in black china, one with a matador and flashing cape, one with a senorita behind a spread fan. They didn't have lampshades and they were pretty ugly, but Cal thought Christie might like them. The only piece of furniture was a dark wood end table with tapered legs and a small drawer. He remembered his grandfather using it for the *TV Guide* magazine he got in the mail each week.

Cal dragged the items down the stairs, then cleaned them up as well as he could. He put them in the office until she could look at them.

At lunchtime, he opened the new refrigerator for sandwich fixings only to find fruit, vegetables and baby formula crowding out his food. He was surprised that Christie cooked, but she'd told him she'd taken classes. Of course she had. Her mother wouldn't have cooked. They probably had a cook, or at least a housekeeper. That was Christie's world, a far cry from what he could offer on this ranch.

Although he wasn't into the bank any longer and there was income coming in from the leases, he wasn't going to get rich as a rancher. If... *When* he restored the Herefords, he'd have a lot of debt. What then?

A man needed to provide for his family or he wasn't a man. A real man didn't let his woman provide most of the money for the family upkeep, for the children's education, for even the clothes on their backs. How could he provide all that and still keep the ranch true to its roots?

You can't, a voice inside him advised. He didn't want to hear that, so he slammed the refrigerator and headed out the back door.

In town, he drove by the Burger Barn, continued on down to the parking in the vacant lot behind McCaskie's garage. James might be in the Burger Barn having lunch, as was his habit.

Cal had already heard the story of how James used to walk by Clarissa's House of Style, where his wife, Sandy, had worked last December, to check her out. Back then, Cal had been told, her hair had been bright red and she'd gone by the name of Scarlett. That must have been a sight.

Thankfully, she'd come to her senses and now all that remained were some red streaks in her brown hair. Still, Cal had a hard time imagining his conservative lawyer, who was his brother's age, falling for such a wild woman.

Yeah, people probably said the same thing about Christie's getting involved with him. What did a beautiful, rich society widow like Christie see in a veteran and rancher who didn't even have a college degree, who had more heritage than money?

Well, he couldn't control what other people thought, he told himself as he opened the door to the Burger Barn and looked around. Sure enough, James was sitting at a table by himself, chowing down on a nice, juicy burger. It looked and smelled so good that Cal went over and ordered one for himself.

"Hey, James," Cal said while he waited for his order. "Mind if I ask you a question?"

"No, have a seat."

"How difficult is it to change a baby's name on a birth certificate?"

James swallowed, then wiped his mouth with a paper napkin. "Not hard unless it's challenged. If both parents make a reasonable request, it's almost always granted."

"Good. I'm going to try to talk Christie into changing the baby's name to what it should be—Calvin Peter Crawford V."

"Let me know if I can help. Have you heard from Troy and Raven?"

"Not yet. I guess they're getting settled."

"How's Christie doing?"

"She's fine. She's in Fort Worth or somewhere shopping for the old motel."

"We're really excited about the Sweet Dreams opening again. The town needs a motel."

"I guess, but it would be simpler and less expensive to just build a new one."

"Ah, but she wants the character of the old place. And, I've got to admit, a lot of folks agree with her. My mother's generation, for example, have good memories of the motel when it was newer and provided good, clean, reasonable rooms for folks coming into town for visits."

"We walked through the place the other day. It seems like a lot of work."

"There's nothing wrong with hard work. You, of all people, should know that."

"Yeah, I guess. My father was a hard worker."

"So are you."

"Not so much anymore. I don't have a lot to do with a handful of Herefords and a bunch of bison who stand around and eat grass. You can barely herd the damn things!"

James chuckled. "I can see where that might be difficult. They're pretty big."

"Too big. They shouldn't be at the Rocking C."

"I've heard that people drive out there to see them."

Cal shook his head. "Maybe I'll start charging a fee."

"Stranger things have happened."

"You've got that right." He retrieved his order, then the two of them ate in silence. Then it was time to get back to work. What little work he had to do. What he needed was a project to keep his hands and his mind busy.

JUST BEFORE DARK ON FRIDAY, Christie pulled to a stop beside the house. Her SRX was laden with all kinds of treasures, Peter was sound asleep and she had a suspicion that Darla, whom she'd dropped off at the Maxwell ranch on the way in, was almost as tired as she was. The trip had been a huge success, as evidenced by the hole in her bank account.

Riley came bounding out to greet her as soon as the car stopped. He was followed closely by Cal.

She put her fingers to her lips as he approached. "Peter is asleep. If we're careful, he'll probably stay down for the night."

"Do you want to carry him in? I'll start unloading your… stuff." He cast a disbelieving glance at all the packages and boxes filling the back.

"Just my suitcase, diaper bag and purse," she said as she gently opened the rear door. She unlatched Peter carefully and slid him into her arms. "I have to find a place to store the rest of my stuff until I can secure the motel."

By the time she got Peter to bed, Cal had placed her purse and diaper bag on the table. "Did he stay asleep?"

"Yes, he's tired. So am I. Shopping can be very exhausting."

"I wouldn't know about that."

No, he probably wouldn't. He'd already told her that he bought his clothes "wherever" and the rest of his things "local, if possible" and hardly ever went to "the city."

"I don't suppose there's a storage facility in town, is there? I should have already checked, but it wasn't on my list."

"There's one in Graham, but not in Brody's Crossing. How much do you need to store?"

"Lots. I'm having the furniture shipped via a local delivery service I know in Fort Worth. They'll go around and pick up all the items at the different stores and deliver them wherever I say. I just need to find a place."

"There's some room in the barn, but I'm not sure it's enough space."

"Maybe I could look at it later, or in the morning."

"Sure." Cal looked around the kitchen. "So, have you had dinner?"

"We ate in Fort Worth before we left. How about you?"

"I had a sandwich earlier. Um, do you want something to drink?"

"I'd love a glass of wine. And I'd love to sit down with an adult and talk about something other than babies, bottles and diapers."

"I can handle that," Cal said, opening the refrigerator. "There's a bottle of white wine in here."

"That's fine. Help yourself if you'd like. I'm going to prop my tired feet up and relax." She stopped before she'd taken two steps. "You know, I'm not even sure that you like wine." Just one more thing they didn't know about each other.

"It's okay. I like red wine better than white."

"I'll bring some reds out next time," she offered, smiling at him. Maybe she could teach him a little about wine so he'd learn what type he preferred. If they were in Fort Worth, she might even suggest a fun wine class.

But they weren't in Fort Worth. And besides, Cal wasn't the "fun wine class" sort of guy. He would probably take learning about wine very seriously.

"Christie?" he said before she'd taken three steps into the living room.

She backtracked and peered around the corner. "Yes?"

"I really missed you," Cal confessed. "And Peter, too."

She smiled at him. "We missed you, too. It's good to be back."

Chapter Nine

Christie decided to rent a storage unit in Graham on Monday morning rather than try to cram her furniture and accessories into the dusty barn. She did appreciate the offer, though, and gave Cal a quick kiss to show her gratitude. He, being a man, tried to turn it into more, but she'd used an appointment as an excuse to run out of the barn. Now she was driving back from Graham with plenty of time to think about her situation.

Being around Cal was starting to be a problem. She knew that pursuing a physical relationship before they addressed their emotional issues wasn't a good idea, but was having a hard time convincing her body to agree. Last night she'd made sure they didn't snuggle together on the couch, although that's what she really wanted to do. Especially when she had relaxed and finished her glass of wine. She'd really wanted to put her bare feet in his lap and have him start by rubbing her feet…and maybe much more.

What a recipe for disaster. That man would have worked his way north faster than she could say, "Whoa, cowboy"—not that she could guarantee she'd say those words.

In the long term, could they find mutual values and goals on which to establish a marriage? Could they raise Peter together? Sometimes they were so compatible, but other times…Cal seemed to mistrust her intentions. He also didn't like the idea that she had more money in the bank than he earned from the ranch. She wasn't keeping score, but apparently he was.

Christie pulled into the motel parking lot. Only a few trucks were there, and she realized it was lunchtime. Grabbing the flooring samples, she took them to the open units to make her final decision.

Sunlight streamed through the dirty, aluminum-framed windows. The temperature was nearing ninety and there was no breeze. Christie placed the laminate floor samples and the retro-look tile squares on the floor and stepped back. Now that she had picked out most of the furniture, she could make a decision. She hoped.

"Hi, pretty lady," a masculine voice said from behind her.

She whirled around and saw Leo Casale standing in the doorway. "You scared me!"

"Sorry," he said with a grin, not looking sorry at all. "I drove by looking for my sister."

"I haven't seen her." Christie took a deep breath and looked out the window. "Only a few of her guys are working during lunch."

"It's not that important. So, are you deciding on flooring?"

"Trying to. I bought eight bedrooms this past week during my shopping trip. I still need two more, but I also need to decide on the flooring that will go best with all of them, or decide which to use in which room."

"You're going to save money if you can go with one flooring choice. Plus, if there's ever damage, like a water leak or vandalism in a room, you can have extra flooring that will work in any room."

"That's a good point. I'd been thinking mostly about how

it looks. What kind of feeling it might provoke in the people staying here."

"Linoleum was really popular back then, but if you're going for a more homey look in each room, which I suppose you are since you bought individual bedroom sets, you might want a wood or wood look. Most homes from the 1940s through the 1960s had hardwood floors."

Christie folded her arms and smiled at Leo. "You are just a fount of information."

He grinned back. "I've learned about a lot of things since I started running the hardware store."

"Oh? How long have you had the store?" She'd assumed he'd been doing it for a long time, since Toni had mentioned that she and Leo had moved to Brody's Crossing when they were small children and had gone to school there.

"About four years." He walked over the flooring and examined the samples. "How about this color?" he asked, cutting off her opportunity to ask any more personal questions. Leo obviously didn't think his previous life was interesting, but there was something about him that didn't say "small-town hardware store owner."

"That's one of my favorites," she said, standing beside him. "I also like this one," she said, nudging a warm golden oak with her toe. It seemed very old-fashioned.

"It's fairly yellow. Will it go with everything?"

"Maybe not," she said, frowning. "This is hard."

Leo laughed. "You asked for it. This is one of the biggest projects in Brody's Crossing in several years."

"Really?"

"Sure. We opened the old farmers' market last year, but that just involved repairs to an existing wood frame."

"I'm very encouraged by the progress." Which was an understatement. She couldn't wait to see all the furniture and accessories in each room. She was especially fond of the two lamp bases and the table that Cal had found in the attic. She doubted that she would use them in the actual motel rooms. More than likely, they would go in the owner's suite. Later, when Peter was older, she could explain that those items came from his great-grandparents' house.

She needed to ask Cal if there were any photos of his family that she might copy. As a matter of fact, having vintage photos of different families in Brody's Crossing was a good idea for the motel rooms. It would give each room a personal flare.

"Where's the baby today?"

"Back at the ranch with Darla Maxwell. She's babysitting for me this summer."

"Good for her." He glanced at the big watch—the kind with all sorts of bells and whistles—on his wrist. "I'd better get going. It was good seeing you, Christie."

"Same here, Leo."

Once he was gone, she looked one more time. Leo was right. The medium-dark walnut laminate would look good with everything she'd bought. She gathered the samples and went down to the office. After writing a note to Toni, Christie left everything on the check-in desk for her contractor.

She went to the café for lunch, saw "the girls" and got a lead on who might have retro furniture, then headed home. Peter would probably be asleep, but that was okay because she needed to make some phone calls. She had a delivery to schedule and she needed to find someone, preferably local, who could do some furniture repairs and refinishing.

"DID YOU SEE YOUR PARENTS while you were in Fort Worth?" Cal asked to make conversation as they finished dinner that night. It was his night to cook and he'd fixed hamburgers on the charcoal grill out back.

"No, I was too busy shopping. I talked to my mother a few days before I came to town, though."

"So, you're not real close to them?" She hardly ever talked about her mother, and never her father, except to mention his hotel business.

"Not particularly. You might as well know that I married the first time—well, the only time—mostly to irritate my father. My husband, Aldo, was a bona fide playboy. He was fun and flashy, good-looking and completely irresponsible." She shook her head and smiled, but her lip trembled a little. "My father hated him on sight. The fact that Aldo's family was rich didn't even impress him. So, I moved to Europe and only spoke to my family occasionally. I partied and had fun—for about six months. Then it got a little old. I ended up spending most of my time at the villa near Florence, or with my friends when they visited."

"Sounds like something I'd read about in one of those celebrity magazines. I can't even imagine that kind of life."

"It looks a lot better in those glossy photos than it feels like in real life," Christie said, her voice sad. She seemed to visibly shake off her bad memories. "A few good things came from living in Italy. I learned to cook. I learned how to choose wines, which was something my father had always done when we went out. He's very traditional. He believes men should make decisions that impress others, while women should have more tedious duties, like making social arrangements."

Cal nodded. He pretty much understood that sort of thinking. At the Rocking C, his father hadn't known a thing about wines or entertaining, but he had known what he thought was women's work versus a man's responsibilities.

"My parents used to argue about the fact my father didn't do anything around the house and wouldn't hear of my mother giving advice or help outside." They'd had some terrible fights, conducted in fierce whispers at times. The arguments almost always ended with his father storming out of the house and his mother crying.

"A long time ago, my father had a room with a cot and a little table in the barn. That was his 'doghouse' when they had fights. He'd go out there, drink a few beers and listen to the radio. Or if it was daylight, he'd saddle up and ride fences. Mostly, I think he brooded."

"That's sad. My parents don't fight. Arguments are much too uncivilized. They just get very silent, sometimes for weeks. Or Daddy will go on an extended trip visiting the various hotels, and Mother will spend lots of time at the spa."

"Different situations, but same problems, I suppose."

"I suppose. So, we both come from dysfunctional families."

"And people say we have nothing in common," he said with a smile, trying to lighten the mood.

"I'm sorry your mother passed away so young, especially when she and your father had an unhappy marriage."

His smile faded. "She didn't pass away all that young. I guess I gave you the wrong impression when I said she was gone. She left us the spring before I graduated from high school. Troy was fourteen." None of them had understood his mother's desertion at the time. Hell, he still didn't.

"Oh. I'm sorry. I didn't realize."

"It's old news."

"Still, that's so sad."

"She was moody. We learned later that she was probably bipolar, but she never went to the doctor or the shrink. She didn't take medication." He shrugged. "If she'd gotten some treatment, maybe she would have been able to cope better with life at the ranch."

"Do you think that's what made her leave?"

"Hell, I don't know. Mostly, I remember that my mother

was unhappy. She coddled my brother more than she did me, I guess because my father expected more from me. Her leaving hit him a lot harder than it hit me."

"And he was younger. Still, that must have been traumatic for all of you."

Cal shrugged again. "We got by." His father had gotten more angry, more dedicated to the ranch. He'd withdrawn from everyone, since some of the single women in town thought he might like a little female comfort. That was the last thing his father had wanted.

Christie sighed, then started gathering the dishes. He picked up the glasses. The baby was busy pushing crumbles of cheese around on his tray.

"You know that ranch life isn't for everyone," he said as they stood beside the sink. "I get up long before dawn, regardless of the weather, seven days a week. A rancher has to think about his stock all the time. It's not an easy thing for a woman to accept, especially if she's not used to the life."

Christie nodded. "I can understand your point. Do you ever see yourself doing something besides ranching?"

"Never." Not only was this what he'd been brought up to do, it was is what he wanted. He'd missed few things while on active duty, but the Rocking C...he'd thought about the ranch every day, almost every hour.

"Well, I believe that everyone should pursue their dreams. If yours is here, on this ranch, I can understand that. I'm just trying to find out what mine is."

"How will you know when you find it, if you don't know what it is?"

She took a deep breath and thought about his question for a moment. "I know that part of my dream has been realized in having a child. I think perhaps that could be my greatest calling, but it's not everything. I need to create something else. That's partly what the motel renovation is about—creating something. It's not what I expected or planned when I first drove into Brody's Crossing, but it seems so right. I don't know how to explain all my dreams, my goals. I just need…more. Something beyond my precious baby and my project."

"You're used to so much, Christie. There's not a lot 'more' for you here, is there?"

"I'm not sure, Cal, on a personal level," she said, placing her hand on his chest, right above his heart, "but when I find it, I'll know." She looked up at him and repeated softly, intently, "I'll know."

THE NEXT DAY, Christie lingered over a second cup of coffee at the kitchen table while Darla played with Peter on the floor in the living room. Cal should be in from morning chores at any time, and she had an idea to get him away from the ranch for lunch.

After last night's conversation, she suspected that Cal could retreat into this ranch much as his father had. This was Cal's sanctuary. Yet with all the changes, he seemed a little lost at times. At other times, he showed a temper, which Christie assumed had to do with his experiences in the war, and the changes to the ranch. Life-changing events had happened that were beyond his control, and that was hard for most people to handle. And for someone who was accustomed to being in control of his life, it must be very difficult.

She was updating her to-do list on her BlackBerry when Cal opened the back door and strode into the room. He was a quiet man, but seemed to charge the air wherever he went. At least, he charged the air around *her*. And more. Since she'd been living at the ranch, spending more time with him, she'd had some time to compare the man she'd known a year and a half ago to the man who lived on this ranch.

In some ways, they were two different people—urban Cal versus rancher Cal. But now she recognized many of his inherently good qualities. He was very dependable and responsible—sometimes, to a fault. He was also kind, in a reserved way, to everyone. Even to the dog he claimed he didn't want. He complained about people wanting to do things for him, yet he was gracious when the town planned an event to welcome him home. His loyalty lay with this ranch, his family and his community.

She needed to figure out where she and Peter fit into that allegiance hierarchy.

"How are things at the barn?" she asked.

"Fine. There's a new bison calf. It's nearly as red as a Hereford, but it will turn dark later."

"How did you learn about them?"

"Troy left me some information from the original breeder."

"That's good. I would expect the Internet would be a good resource, too."

"There's conflicting information, depending on what Web site you look at. There are apparently different strategies for raising bison. For example, if you're going to show them, they need to be big. However, if you're raising them naturally for meat, they need to be grass-fed and leaner."

"How about colleges? I'll bet Texas A & M would have good resources."

"Maybe. Honestly, I was hoping I could get rid of the damn things and get cattle back in here, but Troy made such an investment in them, plus contracting with the new butcher in town for the extra bull calves, that I'm stuck with them for a while."

"I think they're cute. I took Peter out to see them the other day and he laughed and pointed at them."

Cal got a glass and filled it with water from the faucet. He never drank her bottled water. "They're too different from cattle. You can't work them with horses and they don't even fit in most cattle chutes for worming and vaccinations."

"Have you eaten bison meat?"

Cal shrugged. "Yeah. It's okay." He finished his water and placed the glass beside the sink.

"I was wondering if you'd like to go to lunch with me. Also, I wanted to stop by the church to see if they have any of the retro furniture that Ida and Clarissa thought they might have taken in years ago."

Cal leaned his butt against the cabinets, stretching out his long legs. His boots were dusty and his jeans a bit frayed at the hem. He looked sexy as hell. "Are you going by the motel?" he asked.

"Hmm? Maybe. I left samples for Toni yesterday, and I thought I'd follow up with her on our construction timeline."

"So, you made a decision?"

"Yes! I went yesterday, placed the samples on the floor, and then Leo Casale suggested the walnut laminate and—"

"Leo Casale was at the motel?" His hands gripped the edge of the countertop.

"He stopped by to see Toni, but she wasn't there."

"I'll bet he saw your Cadillac and decided to see *you*."

"You are so full of it!" she said with a laugh.

"I'm a man and I understand these things."

"Mmm-hmm. Well, he was very helpful."

"I'll just bet he was."

"As a matter of fact," she said, just to give Cal more motive to go with her, "I might stop by his store to look at hardware options for the new cabinets."

"Isn't it a little early to do that? Besides, Toni can get samples for you."

"Oh, I hate to ask her to do something so trivial when I can just go by Leo's place and check them out."

Cal pushed away from the cabinet. "I'll be ready to go in half an hour."

Christie smiled and added "hardware samples" to her BlackBerry to-do list.

CAL WAS SURPRISED that Christie wanted to go to Graham to pick up a few things and satisfy a sudden craving for lasagna. Eating in a restaurant where people didn't know you was a relief he hadn't expected.

He should have probably stayed to work with Miguel and John, who were digging a new stock tank so the pasture could be divided once they separated the bull calves from the heifers. Unlike cattle, male bison weren't usually castrated because it didn't improve the meat and it was damned dangerous. They'd eventually go to market, but bison matured slower and he was stuck with them for a couple of years. Digging a new tank was dirty work, and since he'd rented only one backhoe, there wasn't much for him to do except direct the guys or use a shovel. He might as well spend some time with Christie.

After shopping at Wal-Mart, he carried a fancy new fax machine, portable plastic file drawers and lots of other supplies to her car. Her turquoise wraparound sundress and strappy sandals with little rocks and jewels didn't seem very practical for carrying loads. Her blond hair was pulled away from her face with a wide headband, and she looked awfully good walking next to him.

She'd asked him for family photos of his grandparents and perhaps his father during the 1950s and 1960s. She was asking others, as well. He didn't know if there were any photos she might want, so he planned to give her the whole box and she could go through them. He didn't have any interest in reliving the past.

"How do you suppose I could find a furniture refinisher?" she asked him as she buckled up in the parking lot.

He almost answered "the hardware store" before realizing that she might take that as an invitation to go to Casale's in Brody's Crossing. "Here in Graham or back home?"

"I don't care. The furniture is going to be in storage here, but it will need to go to the motel."

"You might check with James Brody's father. He's retired and had a minor stroke a while back, but he does good woodworking. He might know someone else, too. And Rodney Bell and Burl Maxwell will know almost everyone. Burl teaches at the high school, but he's off for the summer."

"Those are good leads. I'll give them a call, but I don't know Mr. Brody's number."

"I'll give James a call and ask his father to call you." When Christie had first moved here, Cal had resented the way she'd spent her money. Flaunted it, he thought. Now he realized she didn't care much about the money. She simply had a straight-forward approach to getting what she wanted done.

Of course, she was a bit spoiled into thinking she could get whatever she wanted.

"Thanks. You're a great asset," she said.

"Yeah, that's me." He was a regular Yellow Pages of people and places.

"And a good lunch companion."

"You do most of the talking."

"Do you mind?"

"Hell, no. I'd rather listen to you than my own boring voice."

"I don't think you're boring, and I could listen to you for hours."

She'd shocked him with that remark. "You could?"

"Of course. You probably think what you have to say isn't profound, but it's all new to me. Your views, your knowledge, are different from mine. We've experienced different life events, and the idea of growing up in a small, supportive town is fascinating to me."

"It's just a normal town."

"I don't know about that. The people here are so nice."

"I suppose. They're the people I've known most of my life."

"Believe me, they're nicer than a lot of people I've known all my life."

He could believe that, growing up as she had with rich folks in a larger town. Plus, her parents didn't seem like the "warm and fuzzy" type—not that his were, either. Well, his mother had been at times, and sometimes she'd almost smothered people with her hugs and neediness. He'd retreated then, finding comfort in his chores around the ranch.

"So," he said, "what are we doing now?" He hoped she'd gotten that notion of going to the hardware store out of her head, especially dressed as she was. Leo Casale did not need to see her looking this attractive.

"Weren't we going to stop by the hardware store?"

Cal groaned. "No, I don't think we agreed to that."

Christie smiled as she drove north toward Brody's Crossing. "I guess we'll go to the church, then."

Chapter Ten

Christie was very excited to discover that a family the church had helped ten years ago might still have some of the furniture that had come from the old Crawford house. The church secretary told them the family had moved into a large, unfurnished house in the country after a fire and that they were likely the kind of people who "never threw anything away."

Because it was getting late in the afternoon, however, she and Cal decided not to go out there today. Besides, having another errand to run would get him away from the ranch another day and take his mind off the changes he wanted to make.

Raven owed her for distracting Cal, she thought as she drove under the Rocking C arch. "When are Raven and your brother marrying?"

"I guess that's coming up in a few weeks."

"You don't have your airline ticket?"

"Um, no. I think Troy is taking care of it." He frowned, then added, "You and Peter should go also."

"Oh, I don't think we… I mean, it's just a small family wedding, isn't it?"

"I suppose, but you're family. Peter is definitely family. He's a Crawford. He should be at his uncle's wedding."

She hadn't thought about family from that angle. Peter did

have a whole family of living people. Not just those Crawford ancestors she'd talked to Cal about. Peter might even have cousins someday soon. What a wonderful idea! She was an only child and knew she'd never be an aunt unless she married someone with siblings.

"Let me see what I can do about airfare," Christie said.

"You'll need to get details from Raven or Troy."

"I can handle that."

Cal seemed tense as she stopped the SRX by the back door. "I don't want you paying for everything. It's just not right."

"I promise I won't pay for everything." She had a plan that didn't involve paying for much at all. If you didn't count family obligations, that is.

When they entered the back door, Peter was crying. "I'm glad you're home," Darla said. "He's really cranky, and he's running a slight fever."

"Oh, baby," Christie said as she rushed to Peter. "Do you think he has a cold or the flu? Or some other infection?"

"I think he's just teething, but I'm not a doctor," Darla said.

Riley paced the floor, whining.

"You think he needs to go to the doctor?" Cal asked.

"No, not unless his fever goes up or he gets sick to his stomach," Darla said.

"The baby book says that they can get a fever while teething," Christie said, holding Peter close.

"I've rubbed some analgesic on his gums, and tried to get him to use his teething ring. He's pretty grumpy despite that. You might want to give him some baby Tylenol or whatever you use. I thought I'd wait until you came home. He hasn't been crying for very long."

"That's okay. Yes, we should give him some Tylenol." Peter had been fussy before when Christie was with him. She'd never been gone and come home to find him crying with a fever.

"Would you like me to stay?" Darla asked.

Christie turned to look at Cal. He looked concerned about Peter, and she doubted that he knew what to do any more than she did. "No, that's okay. We appreciate the offer, but you go ahead. We'll take Peter to the doctor if his fever goes up." At least, Christie hoped there was a doctor in Brody's Crossing or somewhere close.

Darla gathered up her purse and waved goodbye as Christie bounced Peter and walked with him. Then she went into the bedroom and found the eyedropper bottle with the lavender liquid that she'd used only once before. "Peter is usually a healthy baby," she told Cal, who stood in the doorway.

"I believe you. Here, I'll hold him while you dose him."

"Dose him? He's not a calf!"

"I know that, babe," he said gently. "He'll be better once he gets some medicine."

Christie rocked Peter and gave him a bottle while Cal did his evening chores. Riley curled up on the braided rug and kept one eye open and one ear cocked, as if listening for the baby's cries. Peter fell into a restless sleep, but his fever was down by seven o'clock that night. Christie grabbed a bite to eat and changed into more comfortable clothes—a soft T-shirt and cotton knit shorts. Her sundress was badly wrinkled and had some formula stains on it.

"How's he doing?" Cal asked after he finished some work in his office. They met in the hallway and spoke softly so they wouldn't wake Peter.

"Better, I suppose. We'll see how well he sleeps tonight."

"You should relax," Cal said, placing his hands on her shoulders. He kneaded her sore muscles and she let out a groan when he hit a sensitive spot. "Come and sit down on the couch."

"Will you rub my shoulders some more?"

"I sure will."

"Okay, then." He took her hand and she let him lead her into the living room. The sun hadn't set yet and she was already sleepy. The couch looked way too comfy.

"I'll, er, sit on the ottoman," she said, "and you sit on the couch. That way, you can massage my shoulders."

She settled back and let him work magic with his strong hands. Slowly, the stress of worrying about Peter faded away and she sank back against Cal's warm chest. Her head fell to the side, against his shoulder, and by the time she realized he was no longer massaging her tight muscles, he was kissing her neck. Which also felt awfully good…

"Are you taking advantage of my extremely lethargic state to put the moves on me, cowboy?"

"Probably," he said between kisses. "Do you mind?"

"Um, no, I don't think I do."

"Okay, then. Just relax."

Christie closed her eyes and leaned back. She felt very lazy as Cal's hands moved from her shoulders to her upper arms, then her stomach. Slowly, they slid up, until he cupped her breasts through the thin cotton of her T-shirt. All her senses went on alert, but she didn't object.

It had been so long since he'd touched her this way. And even then, not in this way. Not so slow and…she didn't even have a word for how she felt. Homey. Comforted. Yet excited.

He rolled her nipples between his fingers and she tensed, moaning. She wanted to lie quietly and let him work his magic, but she also wanted to touch and kiss him. She made herself remain still while he cupped her breasts and pulled her closer.

Her head rolled to the other side, against his neck, and she kissed him there. Their breathing seemed loud in the silent room, in the quiet house. The setting sun bathed the walls and ceiling in muted yellow and pinkish-orange as Cal warmed her from the inside out.

She raised her arms and caressed him wherever she could touch. His neck, his hair, his stubbled cheeks. When her breasts felt so sensitized she couldn't stand any more, she twisted on the ottoman. Cal immediately turned her and dragged her onto the couch.

He kissed her as if he would never let her up. And she didn't care. If this wasn't right, she didn't know what was; they felt so good together. Making out, making love, wasn't about their past or their future, but right now. And, oh, she wanted right now.

His hand wandered to the loose leg of her shorts and she held her breath while he found that lonely place between her thighs. "Yes," she breathed when he touched her there. She arched her back as her fingers dug into the muscles of his upper arms.

"I want you so much," he said against her ear. "So much."

"Yes," she breathed again, reaching for the hem of his shirt, pulling it from his jeans.

"We need… I need to get…protection," he said as she ran her nails up his back. "From the bedroom."

She moaned and held him tighter. She didn't want to let him up for even a minute. What were the odds that she could get pregnant again, when she never could before?

It took only one weekend with this man to conceive Peter, the voice of reason said through the sensual haze in her brain.

"Okay. Not yet," he said roughly, and slid her panties to the side.

She jerked against him, her heart hammering. Yes, oh, yes, she wanted to shout. But they were being quiet for some reason she couldn't quite remember at the moment. Something important… And then her mind went blank and she arched off the couch, clutching Cal, calling his name, shaking as a tsunami of a climax hit her broadside and carried her under.

"Christie," he moaned, holding her tight through the aftermath. His heart hammered hard against her, and his erection strained against her hip as he lay partially on her.

"Now. Protection," she managed to say.

This time *he* groaned in protest. She would love to reach down, caress him, take him into her body and the consequences be damned. But she knew she shouldn't. She should be careful. Which was difficult when every sense was struggling to drown herself in him.

And then she heard Peter cry out, and she remembered where they were and why they were on the couch. And she changed from lover to Mommy in a heartbeat. She pushed Cal aside and leaped from the couch as Riley ran into the room, coming to get her, telling her that the baby was awake and unhappy.

IN THE DARKNESS of the night, Cal tossed and turned, unable to get comfortable or make his mind go blank. He was frustrated—again—and worried about the baby and Christie. None of them was getting much sleep. He heard the floor creak as she walked with Peter. Through the wall, he heard her faint, slightly off-key singing. "Rock-a-bye Baby" blended with some other songs he didn't recognize.

He remembered his mother singing to Troy when he was a baby, and rocking him. Cal didn't want that memory to intrude. He rolled over and pulled the pillow over his head. The old memories should go away and stay away. They were worthless. They didn't change anything. There was no need to long for something you couldn't have. He should be satisfied with what he had: the ranch, Christie, a son.

Cal fell into a fitful sleep later that night and slept for

several hours. He thought perhaps Christie and the baby had also because he didn't hear them through the wall. The incoherent bits and pieces of a dream that had wakened him faded, as did his pounding heart. Taking a deep breath, he swung his legs over the side of the bed.

He stayed that way for a while, listening to the house. All was quiet. He glanced at the clock beside the bed, got up and headed for his bathroom.

It was nearly time to get up, anyway. So what if he'd had only a few hours' sleep? He'd gone on less in Afghanistan, and he'd had plenty of rough nights during calving season or bad weather. As he'd told Christie the other day, a rancher's life wasn't easy. If you wanted a regular job, you might as well move to the city and apply at the local assembly plant or something equally exciting.

He washed his face and hands, then went back to his bedroom to get dressed. He hadn't had time to pull on his jeans over his boxers when he heard the baby cry out.

Rushing toward the room, his only thought was that he wanted to see what was wrong. Had the fever spiked? Was he in pain? A night-light revealed the crib and bed, with Christie pushing her hair back from her eyes and sitting up. She looked beat.

"I'm sorry he woke you," she whispered, swinging her legs over the side of the bed.

"I was already awake. I'll get him up. You rest."

"He probably needs a diaper change, a bottle and some more drops."

"Okay." He'd gotten a lesson in diaper changing, including using that diaper disposer thing that seemed like a lot of work. But he wasn't sure about bottles yet. How did you know how much to give them and when? "I'll do the diaper if you'll get the bottle."

"Oh," she said, wobbling as she stood up. "Okay, if you're sure."

"I'm sure. I can do this."

Peter squirmed and fussed a little. Cal took him over to the bed and laid him on the changing pad. Christie had everything lined up beside it, close but out of reach of baby hands, she'd told him. "Don't put the dirty diaper within reach of the baby," she'd emphasized, and Cal could see where that could be a real problem.

By the time she got back into the room with the bottle, Cal had taken off the wet diaper, cleaned up all the little boy parts and put on a clean diaper. He picked up the baby and held him against his shoulder. "He's good to go," he told Christie. "He doesn't feel all that hot to me."

She stood beside him and placed a hand on the baby's forehead. "No, he doesn't. Maybe he just needs a bottle."

"I can do it."

"Cal, I don't want to disrupt your morning."

"The animals won't mind if I'm a few minutes late."

"Are you sure?"

"Of course. You lie down and rest a while. I'll feed him the bottle."

"Take a burp cloth," she said, handing him one of the little terry-cloth towels she kept around the house. "He dribbles, especially when he's tired."

He took the baby into the living room and settled in the recliner, which was far and away the most comfortable chair in the house. Peter snuggled right up and latched onto the bottle as if he didn't mind at all that someone else was feeding him.

"You're gettin' to know your daddy, aren't you?" Cal whispered to the boy. The baby felt really odd, but good, against his bare skin. Christie had told him that the baby book said it was really important to have skin-to-skin contact so the baby felt secure and bonded.

Before long Peter had finished his bottle, dribbled on himself and Cal, grabbed a handful of chest hair and gone back to sleep. With a sigh, Cal settled his elbows more comfortably on the chair arms and closed his own eyes. He wasn't going anywhere for a while.

Not that he wanted to go anywhere. He'd never held a baby this long. He'd never given his son a bottle in the middle of the night or changed his diaper all by himself. A feeling of pride and contentment came over him, pushing away his earlier dark thoughts and shining like a little personal nightlight in his soul.

He understood now what Christie felt when she got that glow on her face, when she held Peter and played with him. This was what it felt like to be a parent. To love a child.

Cal sighed and relaxed in his chair. He would do whatever it took to make this feeling last forever.

WHEN CHRISTIE WOKE, the sun was shining and she felt much more rested. She got up and looked in the crib, but Peter wasn't there. Frowning, she had a vague memory of Cal telling her to go back to sleep and he would take care of feeding the baby. She rubbed her eyes. Yes, she remembered. He'd also changed Peter's diaper. Had that been around five o'clock this morning?

If so, where were they now? She picked up her cell phone and looked at the time display. Nearly nine o'clock. Cal was usually finished with several hours of chores by now, and Peter was barely finished with his breakfast.

She made a quick stop in the bathroom, splashed water on her face and headed out to find her son. And his father.

In the kitchen, she found fairly fresh brew in the coffeemaker, which was a good sign. But Cal and Peter were nowhere in sight. She walked through the other rooms, including Cal's bedroom, which she'd never entered. No one there.

She heard the back door open and Riley's rat-a-tat-tat nails on the vinyl tile. Cal was talking, but she couldn't understand what he was saying. Rushing into the kitchen, she felt as if she'd stepped into an alternate universe.

Cal wore the baby carrier she'd purchased in Fort Worth so she could take Peter with her on the motel job site and still use her hands. Peter was perched like a chubby little teddy bear in front of his daddy, grinning and pumping his little legs and waving his arms. Cal, on the other hand, wore an expression that seemed to say "Don't laugh."

"Um, hi. Peter looks as if he's feeling much better."

"I think so. We're running a little late this morning. We both had a nice nap in the chair."

"I see. Thank you for taking Peter. I also got some good sleep."

"We did chores."

"I see." Something was different. Cal had rarely held Peter or taken the initiative in caring for him. He'd been reluctant, as if he were afraid of doing something wrong. But now, he'd cared for Peter and taken him to the barn and did who knows what. "So, you and Peter are…okay?"

"More than okay. He likes the animals and the chores. We're going to do lots of things together, aren't we, buddy?" He tickled Peter's neck and made him giggle.

"That's…great."

"Hey, do you think I should get a car seat for my truck?"

"I'm not sure where you could put it. Do you have air bags on the passenger side?"

Cal snorted. "No. It's a work truck."

"All the books say that a baby is safest in the backseat."

"Yeah, you've got a point. I'll check on it."

Peter began to fuss. "I imagine he's wet. Would you like for me to unhook him?" she offered.

"Sure. I'll go jump in the shower first, then you can take yours. I assume you've got some errands to run and some business to take care of."

"Yes, I do." She had furniture to track down, photos to arrange for and a project to check on. "Darla should be here soon."

"I'll take care of Peter while you get ready," Cal said, smiling at her. As soon as she managed to get Peter out of the carrier, Cal leaned down and kissed her briefly.

She was so shocked she barely heard Peter's squeals or felt his little hands slapping her shoulder. What had happened between when Cal had awakened at five o'clock and when she'd gotten out of bed the second time?

Shaking her head, she decided to get her morning going fast. She saw the phone numbers Cal had left for her and called Raven in New Hampshire first. While they talked, Christie carried Peter into the bedroom and laid him on the bed.

"When and where is the wedding?" Christie asked after they'd exchanged greetings.

"It's in Marathon. That's in the Florida Keys, on July the twelfth. Are you coming?"

"Cal said that Peter and I should come, but I'm not sure yet. He's never flown before, and I'm in the middle of the motel renovations." She stuffed his wet diaper into the Diaper Genie and reached for a new one.

"I hope you can come. It would be great to have you there. The wedding will be small, with just my mother and a few friends coming from Manchester. We have a private swim scheduled with the rehabilitated dolphins that morning, and then the ceremony will be overlooking the Gulf at sunset."

"I'm going to see what I can do." She got the clean diaper on with no mishaps.

They chatted for another minute, then Christie ended the call and finished adjusting Peter's clothes.

After they went back into the kitchen, she put him in his high chair to have a cereal bar. While she got his baby yogurt out of the refrigerator, she dialed her father's office. After talking with his efficient and mildly friendly secretary for a minute, she got him on the line. She settled in the kitchen chair, wedged her phone between her shoulder and ear and fed Peter his breakfast.

"Hello, Daddy," she said when he answered.

"Christine. I'm surprised to hear from you. Are you back in Fort Worth?"

She could almost hear the unspoken *"Have you come to your senses?"* question. "No, Peter and I are still in Brody's Crossing."

"What can I do for you, then?"

Again, that unspoken question, *"Why are you calling me?"* or even *"Why are you bothering me?"* "I need to travel to a wedding in July and I'm not comfortable with the idea of taking Peter on a commercial airline." She'd heard horror stories of airlines holding people on planes, at the gate or on the tarmac, for hours and hours. Parents had run out of diapers and formula for their babies. She wasn't going to subject her child to that if she could avoid it.

"A wedding? You're not marrying that cowboy, are you?"

"He's a rancher, not a cowboy, and no, I'm not. This is his brother's wedding. Cal would really like Peter to be there."

"He's just a baby. It's not like he'll remember it."

"No, but there will be photos."

Her father sighed. "I suppose you'd like to use the corporate jet."

"Yes, I would, if you're not using it the weekend of July the twelfth. The wedding is in the Florida Keys."

"I'll have to check my calendar. And with the other executives, of course."

She closed her eyes and summoned patience. Of course, the other executives were more important than his own daughter, now that she no longer worked for the company. "Thank you for checking. I'll look forward to hearing from you."

"Your mother would appreciate a call regarding the planning of the Kimball Art Museum benefit."

Christie inwardly sighed. So, it would be quid pro quo. "I'll call her this afternoon."

"See that you do. And I'll call regarding the jet."

She'd just flipped her phone closed when Darla arrived and took over cleaning Peter after his messy cereal-bar-and-yogurt breakfast. Shortly after that, Cal walked into the kitchen, all clean and smelling great. He wore a pec-hugging U.S. Army T-shirt tucked into soft, faded jeans.

Christie thought of her own tangled hair and wrinkled clothes.

"What's wrong?" he asked.

She must be frowning. Either that, or she looked worse than she thought. "I just got off the phone with my father."

"Oh. Is anything wrong?"

"No. Everything is perfectly normal." Normal for her family, at least. "I'd just forgotten how manipulative he can be."

"I, um—"

"I didn't mean to be negative. It's just that he pushes all my buttons. It's his way or the highway. His rules or he takes his ball and goes home." She shook off the lingering bad feelings. If she wanted the comfort and convenience of the private jet, she'd have to put up with her father's usual high-handed ways. "I'm hitting the shower now. I'll be ready as quickly as possible."

Cal gave her a hug, which felt a little awkward after the intimacies of last night and, yet, was oddly comforting. "Take your time. Sounds like you could use a relaxing shower. Darla and I will take care of Peter."

"Okay." She paused at the doorway and looked back at Cal. "I'm not sure what happened this morning, but I'm happy for you…and Peter."

"Me, too," Cal said with a smile.

Chapter Eleven

Cal missed Peter during the day as he and Christie chased down some old furniture that may or may not have belonged to his grandparents. Still, he enjoyed spending time with her. At first, she was quiet. Cal assumed that was a result of the phone call to her father. He hoped she didn't regret what had happened last night on the couch before Peter had interrupted them. The only thing Cal regretted was that they hadn't finished what they started.

Maybe tonight, he thought as he watched her talk to the weathered, poor couple who lived just off a gravel road in the country. Christie was a shining contrast in her white walking shorts and pale blue bandana-print top that floated around her in the summer breeze and clung to her breasts.

When she saw a dirty old light-wood dresser and headboard stored in a run-down barn beside the rusty trailer where the couple lived, she just about did a happy dance right there in the dusty yard. She paid the owners far more than it was worth, in Cal's opinion, and he helped the man load it into Cal's pickup truck.

"Nine down, one to go," she said joyfully as they drove off.

"Have you found a refinisher yet?" he asked as he pulled

out onto the Farm to Market Road, five miles or so from Brody's Crossing.

"Not yet. That's on my to-do list."

"How's that list coming along?"

"Pretty well." She was quiet for a moment, then added, "I'll let you know as soon as possible about the wedding. I talked to Raven this morning and got details on the ceremony."

After the furniture purchase, they stopped by the community center to post a notice for photos. Christie invited residents to provide copies or original photos from the 1950s and 1960s that she could copy, enlarge and frame for the rooms of the motel. She promised them the originals back and that they would get credit for supplying the photo.

"That's a really nice idea," Cal said as they headed for the truck. "Will they ever get to see the photos on the walls?"

"I'm going to have a big opening party for the people around here and the media from Graham to Dallas. It will be an opportunity for everyone who's interested to see the renovations, plus great publicity just before the opening."

"Another good idea." Although her background in marketing was really paying off, in his opinion, the need for a motel in Brody's Crossing was still unproven. "Let's go eat." He pulled out of the community center and headed for Dewey's. He'd gone out to eat more with Christie in the past two weeks than in the previous two years, but he'd decided that if it made her happy, he'd do it. Today he was renewing his campaign to get her to marry him and stay in Brody's Crossing with Peter forever. He'd be pleasant and keep his opinions to himself.

"We can go back to the ranch if you'd like," she said, placing a hand on his arm as he drove out of the downtown area. "I think there's some chicken left from the night before last."

She'd fixed a fancy dish with chicken breasts and sauce. It

was pretty good, but it wasn't beef. "No, that's okay. We can have it for dinner."

She gave him a confused look but said nothing else, which was fine with him. He wanted to talk to Christie, but half the time, he didn't know what to say. He'd already said too much about certain subjects. Not that he'd influenced her one bit. She'd gone ahead with her plans as if he hadn't even given his unwelcome opinion.

That was probably because she was a strong-willed woman. Well, he couldn't complain about that character trait. He was pretty strong-willed himself, and besides, a woman had to be strong to make it in this world on her own.

Just not strong enough to run off and leave him.

CHRISTIE AND CAL returned to the ranch after lunch so she could get some more calls made and print out some e-mails for her files. Cal mentioned that he wanted to meet with Brian Wilkerson, the man leasing the pasture for the big, fat dairy cows that moved slowly and ate constantly. She'd seen him drive up in his small pickup to milk every morning and night, and feed the cows.

"You're not going to try to get out of the lease, are you?" Christie asked as she grabbed her purse, tote bag and uneaten dessert from Dewey's, which Cal had insisted she needed.

"No, but I remembered that he questioned some chemicals he saw in the barn. It's the whole organic thing. He wanted to make sure that I'm not using them on the pasture where his cows are grazing so we can get an organic certification."

She shut the passenger door. "I buy a lot of organic products for Peter."

He opened the tailgate and pulled the dirty headboard toward him. "That must be one of the big trends that I missed while I was on active duty."

"I suppose. Here, let me help you with that." She reached for the other end of the headboard as he pulled. "I've been using natural products for years, whenever I could."

"Is that why you're so pretty?" Cal asked, resting briefly against the truck-bed wall. His biceps strained against the sleeve of his T-shirt as he rested his arm high against the furniture.

She looked at his smiling face for a moment before she could respond. "Are you flirting with me, Cal Crawford?"

"I believe I am." He grinned wider. "Is it working?"

"I'll let you know…later." First, she'd like to figure out what had come over Cal and why he was suddenly a devoted father and suitor. Was this the real Cal, or was he pretending to be happy and cooperative?

"That sounds like a promise," he said, lifting the headboard from the truck without a problem.

She momentarily lost her train of thought as he carried it into the barn. "I think I'll go tell Darla we're back if you really don't need my help."

"No, I'll get Brian to help me." He smiled at her again. "But thanks for offering, pretty lady."

"You're welcome," she said as she walked toward the house.

Inside, Peter was having a good day. No sign of fever or pain, but he was drooling and his nose was running—more signs of teething. At least he was in a good mood.

So good, that after she made a few phone calls, she decided to take him on a quick trip to the motel. She changed Peter, then grabbed the diaper bag and headed for her car.

"We're going to the motel to meet with Toni for a few minutes," she told Cal as he came in the back door. "She needs me to make a decision on something that's come up."

"Do you want me to go with you?"

"No, that's okay. We won't be gone long." As a matter of

fact, she needed a little time away from Cal. "I'll be back in time for dinner."

His jaw clenched ever so slightly, but then he smiled and said, "Sure. See you then."

She buckled Peter into his seat and drove away from the Rocking C with renewed determination to talk to Cal about what he wanted from their relationship now. He'd made himself perfectly clear when she'd arrived in town—get married for the sake of the baby. But since then, he'd changed several times. He no longer talked about marriage. He was so helpful and a lot less negative than he'd been when he'd learned of her plans for the motel.

But where did they stand personally? Would they have made love the other night if Peter's cries hadn't interrupted them? And if they had made love, how would that have changed their relationship? She couldn't imagine, and what she didn't know always bothered her.

She pulled into the crowded parking lot of the motel a few minutes later. Workers were loading tools into their pickups and a stinky asphalt mixer stood off to one side. A pile of gravel spilled from the walkway onto the parking lot. Christie unlatched Peter and dodged the obstacle course as she made her way to the office.

"Toni," she called out.

"Over here," the contractor said. The sound came from the doorway between the office and the owner's quarters. Years ago, the manager had lived in a unit similar to the rest of the rooms, but Christie knew that she'd need more space if she were living there. Or, if she decided she didn't enjoy actually running the motel and hired a manager, that person would appreciate the extra room, especially if he or she had a child.

Christie walked into the construction zone, sorry that she'd brought Peter when he sneezed. The smell of freshly cut lumber permeated the room.

"We talked about putting the doorway to the other unit right here," Toni said after they exchanged greetings, "but I'm not sure that's the best spot."

"Why?"

"You're limiting the place you can put the bed in either room. You don't want to walk around the bed, especially a king size, to get to the other door."

"Oh, I see what you mean. Where do you suggest we put the doorway, then?"

"I think we should put it near the outside wall, maybe two and a half feet in to give clearance for the door. Also, we might want to build the jams for two doors, just in case you ever want to make this a connecting unit. For example, if the manager didn't need two units, the other one could be rented out."

"Oh, I hadn't thought of that. Yes, let's do it. It won't add but a small amount in construction cost, but gives lots more flexibility."

"Okay, then. I'll make the exact measurements and have my guys make the cuts tomorrow."

"I smelled the asphalt. Did the roofers finish?"

"Yes, it's complete. The outside is coming along nicely, and we've been focusing on the owner's suite and the office so far. How's the furniture shopping coming along?"

"Fantastic! I still haven't found a refinisher, but I have nine out of the ten bedroom sets purchased. Cal and I found one just today out in the country. I believe it may be one from the Crawford house, owned by Cal's grandparents."

"Wow, that's great. You should check with Leo and see if he knows anyone who might have time to tackle that large a project."

"Hmm. Do you have time to talk to Leo?"

"Well, sure. Is there something wrong?"

"No, but I don't want to give Leo any idea that I'm…interested in anything other than a friendly relationship." Cal's jealous attitude had made her think that perhaps Leo or others might consider her neighborly conversations with him as another kind of attention to the attractive man.

"Oh, I think everyone knows you're only interested in Cal."

"I suppose living on his ranch and having his baby would give them that idea."

"Yes, and the way people have seen you two around town. He has never spent that much time away from the ranch."

"Promise me you won't tell anyone this," Christie said, and when Toni nodded, she continued. "Raven asked me to keep Cal busy so he wouldn't try to change the Rocking C back to the way it was before. I know that has frustrated Cal, but he's told me he's not doing anything for two years due to the contracts. I'm trying to keep him busy because he doesn't have the same amount of work to do. He gets bored if he doesn't have chores all day long, and then he starts thinking about the way the ranch was before he left."

"Yes, I know what you mean. I've had some experience— a long time ago, mind you—with someone who got bored and got into trouble."

"Oh? That sounds like a good story."

"It's old news, and hardly matters anymore. He moved away and I've moved on. These days, a nice, boring man would be okay with me," Toni said with a smile, then added, "as long as he's good-looking. And knows how to use a hammer and a nail gun."

Christie laughed. "If I find one hanging around, I'll steer him your way."

"Thanks, although I won't have time for romance until I get your project done."

"Good thinking. It's nice to know I come first."

"I'm a businesswoman first and a politician second, some would say, although campaigning in Brody's Crossing is hardly the same as running for office in a larger town or county-wide. Those two professions don't leave me much time for a personal life."

"I didn't think I had much time, either," Christie said, bouncing Peter on her hip, "and then this one came along."

"Well, as you mentioned, first I'd need to meet someone, and I don't see that happening."

"You never know who's going to walk through the door."

Christie walked through the rooms with Toni before leaving. By then, all the vehicles but Toni's truck and Christie's SRX were gone from the parking lot. Even the stinky asphalt was gone. Only its lingering aroma tainted the air.

This side of town was quiet. If they were in Fort Worth, rush hour would be starting and cars would be whizzing by. Tempers would fray as people tried to get home or to dinner or to happy hour. In Brody's Crossing, the only urgency seemed to be Peter's growling tummy.

"We're going home, baby," she told him, then realized what she'd said. Had she really begun to think of the Rocking C as her home? She wasn't sure. All she knew was that she and Cal needed to talk about what he wanted and what they could agree on together.

CAL WAS RUMMAGING through the pantry when Christie and Peter walked through the back door, looking as if they'd had a good outing. He was glad they were back for several reasons. He'd felt out of his element, trying to supplement her fancy chicken dish, which he was warming in the oven. Maybe she'd have a better idea for vegetables, and he'd be off the hook for dinner.

"Um, that smells good," she said, placing the diaper bag on a chair. "Let me put Peter down to play with his toys and I'll help you."

She put the baby in the living room on the fleecy blanket. Riley greeted him as if he'd been gone for days rather than hours. That dog had sure taken to having Peter around. At first Peter was okay with checking out his toys, but as soon as Christie walked out of the room, he began to cry.

"I'll play with him," Cal volunteered, "if you'll find something additional to serve for dinner." He'd enjoy spending more time with his son.

"Sounds good. Carrying Peter around the job site just about wore out my arms."

"He's big for his age, isn't he?"

"Yes, he is. And heavy, although he's not overweight."

Cal settled on the floor and grinned at the baby. "You're just a big boy, aren't you?"

Peter grinned back, and over the next few minutes, Cal learned how to stack blocks, knock them over and laugh as they tumbled across the floor. Then they played with toy telephones with blinking lights and electronic tones, talking animals and lots of books made out of cloth or vinyl. Cal was amazed that Peter didn't miss his mother. Maybe the baby knew or sensed that Cal was his father. Or maybe he was just easygoing.

"Dinner's ready," Christie said, leaning around the corner.

"Okay. We'll wash up." He took the baby to the bathroom with him, but found washing his hands and the baby's was a difficult task. He needed two more hands. Eventually, he placed the baby tummy-down on the countertop, held him with one hand, and let him splash in the running water. Peter squealed and Cal got splattered. Great. Now he looked as if he'd had a bizarre accident.

"It's okay, buddy," he told the baby as they walked into the kitchen. "We know why I have water all over the front of my jeans, don't we?"

"He got you good, didn't he?" Christie asked, looking all flushed and beautiful. Her hair was slightly disheveled and her cheeks were pink, probably from rushing around the kitchen.

"Yeah." He walked over to Christie, bent down and kissed her lightly. "You look beautiful."

She appeared taken aback. "Yeah?"

Peter squealed. "We both think so."

They ate dinner with occasional interruptions from the baby. Green beans became missiles and egg noodles waved like flags. Riley, thankfully, cleaned up most of the mess before Cal and Christie finished their meal. He'd never realized how grateful he was for that dog.

He helped Christie clean up the dishes, then she put the baby in the tub for a bath. Cal supposed he should learn how to do that also, but not tonight. After his bath, Peter played a little while Cal watched part of the Rangers game, then it was the baby's bedtime.

"Do you think I should try to get him to sleep?" Cal asked.

"If you'd like. He's pretty good about going to bed." She showed him how to fix the bottle, settle in the rocker and turn down the lamp until just the night-light was on. Cal rocked the baby and held him close, comforted by the feel of his warm little body tucked close. To his surprise, Peter fell asleep just as he'd done early in the morning as they'd settled in the recliner. Cal got up and placed him carefully on the crib mattress.

When he returned to the living room a few minutes later, Christie was curled on the couch with a glass of white wine. The box of photos he'd given her to look through was on the ottoman. She looked up and smiled. "You did a good job, Daddy."

"Thanks. How long before he starts talking?"

"It varies. *Da-da* or *daddy* are easy words to say, so he'll probably start saying one of them soon. But sometimes boys speak later, so don't be surprised if he's way over a year when he says anything that sounds like a real word and not just babble."

"Hmm." There must be a good reason boys didn't talk early. They were probably just waiting to have something interesting to say, unlike girls, who could talk for hours about nothing. Still, he couldn't wait until his son could call him "Daddy."

"Do you remember when you asked me what I would have called the baby if he were named Calvin Peter Crawford V?"

"Yes, I do."

"I think Peter would have been a good choice. Or maybe Pete. I think Peter sounds a little formal."

"Really?"

"Yeah." He paused, then asked, "Would you ever consider changing his name to 'the fifth' to carry on the tradition?"

"I don't know, Cal. I accept that it's important to you, and I don't want to be disrespectful to the tradition, but I'd like to have part of my name in his also."

"I just wondered how you felt."

"I promise I'll think about it."

Cal gave Christie time to look through the photos. He tried to concentrate on the game, but as usual, the Rangers had trouble with their pitching and gave up three runs in the fifth. He glanced at her occasionally, then more often as she smiled and held up photos. She seemed very entertained by the family pictures. She finished her wine and placed her glass on the end table, then looked at him, a smile still on her lips.

"What?"

"I'm just watching you."

"I thought you were watching baseball."

"You're more interesting."

She raised an eyebrow. "About that," she said, putting the box on the ottoman. "I wanted to talk to you about...us."

"Couldn't we just pick up where we stopped the other night and not talk?"

"I don't think so."

He stifled the urge to turn back to the ballgame. He didn't want to *talk* about them. He wanted to *show* her that they belonged together. "Why don't I come over there beside you so we can talk more comfortably?"

"Again, not a good idea. I know what you're up to, Cal Crawford. Just talk to me, okay?"

He clicked off the television. "What do you want to know, Christie?"

"I want us to talk about what happened and where we're going with this relationship."

"You know what I want."

"No, really, I don't. I know what you wanted two weeks ago, but that was a gut reaction to learning about Peter." She tilted her head and looked at him. "Wasn't it?"

He felt as if he should cross his arms over his chest and defend his actions. But he'd told himself he'd do anything to hold on to the feelings from last night. Or was that early this morning?

"My suggestion that we get married might have been a knee-jerk reaction to finding out about my nine-month-old son. You shocked me. I wanted to do the right thing."

"Meaning you no longer want to do the right thing?"

"No, that's not what I meant." He took a deep breath to control his temper. "When I realized you weren't going to jump on the marriage offer, I quit asking."

"Cal, I hate to tell you this, but you never *asked* me to marry you. You said we *should* get married and you said you *wanted* to get married. I was rather…inconsequential."

"How can you say that? You were never inconsequential. That's ridiculous. I wouldn't have wanted to marry you if I didn't like you."

She leaned forward. "Cal, this may come as a shock, but I would never get married unless someone loved me and I loved him back. *Like* is just not good enough. I'll never settle again."

"What do you mean, again?"

She closed her eyes. "I married the first time very quickly. We were attracted to each other, but mostly, as I've told you, Aldo was everything my father isn't, and I knew my new husband would drive Daddy crazy. So we married on a whim and I tried to love him. I tried really hard. He told me he loved me, and I think he did, but he loved driving race cars and downhill skiing and paragliding in the Alps more. When he died, I felt so guilty, like if I'd loved him more, he wouldn't have done all those dangerous things."

"I don't think that's the reason he risked his life."

"I know that now, but at the time, I felt really bad."

"So, you want the fairy tale. The perfect man and the perfect life," Cal said. "That rules me out, Christie."

"No! I'm not looking for a fairy tale. On the surface, it looks as if I've already had that. Aldo was handsome, rich and worldly. But he wasn't my Prince Charming. He was just… charming." She hugged her arms and shook her head. "I just want someone to love me for who I am, not who they want me to be or who they think I am. I don't think that's asking too much, but maybe it is."

"It's not asking too much," Cal admitted. While he'd like to convince Christie that they should get married just because they'd made a baby together, he accepted her need to be loved. "You are very lovable."

"I think I'm attractive and I'm smart, but sometimes I'm pushy and strong-willed."

"You're not too pushy. If anything, you're too perfect."

Christie scoffed. "I'm hardly perfect."

"You're beautiful and talented and a great mother. You're

so much that…well, it's kind of hard to believe you're here with me."

"Oh, Cal. I do want to be here. I wouldn't have moved in with you or stayed here if I didn't."

He got up from the chair, his heart pounding, and crossed the room to the couch. They didn't need to say more. They needed each other. He wanted to show her how great she really was. He hadn't done such a good job telling her before. He wasn't a man of eloquent words. He'd been taught that actions spoke louder than words.

Tonight, they both needed action.

He pushed the box of photos out of the way and sat on the ottoman in front of Christie. Framing her face with his hands, he looked into her eyes. "There's no one I'd rather have here with me than you, Christie, even if Peter didn't exist. But, God, I'm thankful he's here, too. I'm grateful that you carried my son and gave birth to him, and that you love him as a miracle and as your child."

"Oh, Cal," she said, tears in her eyes.

"I want you so much," he said, and then he kissed her. Deep, hot kisses, and she kissed him back as though she'd never let him go. Yes, that was the response he sought. *She won't leave me,* he told himself as they sank to the cushions. *She wants to be here, with me, on this ranch. Forever.*

"Make love to me," she said as she slid her hands around him, digging her fingers into his back.

He kissed her throat, her neck, her lips as they sank onto the couch. He hadn't wanted to talk, and thank God it was over, but now everything was better because they'd communicated. Now he knew what Christie wanted. He could make this work.

Their relationship would work. He would see that it did, just as he'd make sure that neither he nor Christie would see the sun rise until both of them were completely satisfied.

Chapter Twelve

Christie welcomed Cal's weight as he pressed her into the cushions. His kiss devoured her and she gave back as good as she got, feeling so close, so…admired, if not loved. His simple but eloquent words had moved her beyond belief.

Finally, he'd accepted her as an individual and not just as the mother of his child. Someone who had walked into his life unexpected and uninvited.

Unwanted.

No, he definitely wanted her. The evidence of his desire pushed between her thighs as he kissed her again and again, as if he couldn't get enough. His slightly calloused, big hands worked magic over her body as he pulled away her T-shirt, cupped her breasts and made her moan in pleasure.

"We are wearing too many clothes," he said.

"Do you want to go into your bedroom? Because I'm thinking the bed would be more comfortable than this couch."

"I have fond memories of you on this couch," he said, nipping her jawline, "but you're right. Bed it is." He pushed away after one last kiss and pulled her to her wobbly feet.

"You do have protection, right?" she asked in a soft voice as he led her down the hall, past the barely open doorway to her bedroom, where Peter slept. She would love to have another child, but not right now. Not when she wasn't sure where her long-term relationship with Cal was headed.

Short term, it was headed to his bedroom.

"Yes, I do," he whispered, pulling her into his room. She reached around and closed the door most of the way, so she could hear Peter if he cried out. So hopefully he wouldn't hear his mommy and daddy making very good, sexy love.

"We need baby monitors," she said.

"Not right now. This moment, we need each other." He encircled her within his arms and held her so tightly she could barely breathe. His hands were everywhere, and before she knew what he was doing, her T-shirt was flung across the room and her shorts pooled on the floor.

"You feel so good," he whispered against her throat. "So damn good."

"How long has it been for you, Cal?" she asked.

He raised his head and loosened his grip enough to look into her eyes. She could barely see him in the dim light coming from the hallway and the outside lights. "You're the last woman I made love to, Christie. There's been no one else."

She touched his lips with her trembling fingers. "Me, too."

Tenderness quickly turned to passion as her words seemed to ignite them. She pulled Cal's T-shirt from his jeans and ran her hands all over his warm, muscular chest, back and arms. Oh, he felt so good. So incredible. Better than before.

"I worked hard to get back into shape," she whispered against his chest, "but I'm not the same as before the pregnancy."

"I don't care how you've changed unless it affects you making love, and even then, we'll work something out."

"I think you could tell from last night that's not the case."

"Hmm—" he said, kissing his way to her collarbone "—good point. I don't think we have a problem."

"No, I don't think so," she whispered as he unhooked her

bra and slid the straps down her arms. Her breasts, slightly larger since the pregnancy, filled his hands. She moaned again as he worked magic on her.

She pushed him to the bed and sank onto the mattress. He followed, unsnapping his jeans, then pulling her panties from her hips. She raised up and pulled down his jeans and boxers, wishing she could see more in the heavy shadows of the bedroom. She'd loved looking at Cal when they'd had their one weekend together. He'd slept gloriously naked and she'd admired every inch of his warrior's body.

Now he had a warrior's scars, she thought, touching his temple as he reached across her for the nightstand. The drawer opened and he pulled out a handful of packets.

"I'll apologize in advance if the first time is too quick," he said, his voice rough with desire. "I'll make it up to you, though. I promise," he said, tearing open a packet.

She slid the condom on him. "I know you will. And don't worry. I have a feeling I'll be right with you, all the way."

"Hold on then, babe. This may be a bumpy ride," he said, pushing his way home. Oh, yes, she thought as he rocked against her, then began a rhythm that brought her quickly to the peak. A very bumpy, wonderful ride.

CHRISTIE GOT UP ONCE during the night to give Peter a pacifier when he cried out in his sleep. He didn't wake up fully, so she crawled back into bed and Cal made love to her one more time. They fell asleep, still entwined, and stayed that way until the alarm clock startled her out of a sound sleep at five o'clock.

"It's still dark," she groaned into his chest. "Can't you train those animals to eat later?"

He chuckled. "In the summer, it's necessary to get your chores done early, before the heat is too great. I need to feed the horses and turn them out, check on that bison calf, fill the water trough and put out new cubes for intestinal parasites. Besides, I'm used to getting up in the mornings. The army didn't let us lounge around all morning on our cots."

He kissed her bare shoulder. "You'll get used to it, too, now that you're going to be a ranch wife."

"A…a what?"

Cal chuckled and headed for the bathroom. "We'll talk about it later. I have to go now or I'm going to spend all morning in bed with you while our animals starve, get worms and kick through the stall walls."

She flopped back onto the pillows. She couldn't think at 5:00 a.m., much less talk coherently, so she might as well go back to sleep. She'd set him straight later, when she got her wits about her. After a couple cups of coffee and a nice warm shower.

WHEN CAL RETURNED from morning chores, Christie was seated at the table, feeding Peter his morning meal of baby yogurt. The baby also had a cereal bar, which he proceeded to stuff into his mouth until Cal was sure he'd choke. Christie had told him not to worry, and, sure enough, Peter always "removed" the excess one way or the other, with his fingers or not.

He had terrible table manners, but she didn't seem worried, so who was Cal to be critical? It wasn't as if he'd grown up eating off fine china and using silver forks and spoons. Still, at some point, the boy needed to learn how tó eat properly.

The scene this morning made him smile. Peter was happy, Christie glowed—and Cal thought he knew why—and even Riley was grinning.

"Good morning," he said, unable to contain his smile. "How's everyone?" He walked into the room and rubbed Peter's soft, light brown baby hair and kissed Christie's cheek.

"We're fine," she said, and he thought he saw a bit of a blush on her cheeks. Or maybe he was just projecting. This morning, he felt like crowing. They didn't have a rooster on the ranch, and he could have taken over the responsibility of welcoming the sun with a big cock-a-doodle-do while standing on a fence post. That's how good he'd felt after making love with Christie and waking up with her in his arms.

"Do you need me to go with you today for any of your errands or appointments?" he asked.

"Um, I don't have much set up yet. I'm still waiting on some callbacks."

"I noticed a sagging fence post. And I think I'm going to have to help Miguel and John with the pump on the stock tank out in the southeast pasture."

"That's okay. I'm going to visit the antique mall in Graham, then work on locating a furniture refinisher. That's my main priority now. I have no idea how long it will take to get the pieces repaired."

"Did you get any calls on another bedroom set or on more old photos?"

"Not yet. Still waiting." She paused, then said, "I looked at the calendar this morning. This weekend is Father's Day." She paused again. "It's your first Father's Day, so we can do whatever you'd like, but I thought maybe you'd enjoy going back to Fort Worth."

His first Father's Day. The first of many. "Back to the 'scene of the crime,' so to speak?" he asked with a grin.

Now he knew she was blushing. "Well, that, and I thought perhaps I should visit my own father. Daddy's not the warm and fuzzy type, but he would probably feel slighted if I didn't make the effort."

"Fort Worth is okay with me, as long as the hands can handle the feeding. I'll check with them today."

"That would be great. We could head out Saturday morning after your chores, if that would be good for you."

"That would be great, babe. We'll have a nice family weekend."

She smiled faintly, then turned back to feeding Peter. "Yes, we will," she said softly.

Cal had never known Christie was so shy. He grinned, shook his head and headed for the shower.

"CAL THINKS we're getting married," Christie told Raven on the phone later that morning. She'd driven to Graham to post an ad for both a furniture refinisher and another bedroom set, since Brody's Crossing didn't have a local newspaper. Now she was sitting by herself in a local tearoom, finishing her second cup of Earl Grey after indulging in an oatmeal-raisin cookie. "I didn't agree. I don't know where he got the idea that I wanted to get married now, just because... Well, you know."

"You slept with him again?"

"Well, yeah. Last night. And now, he's all happy and we're going to Fort Worth for the weekend, and it's his first Father's Day and I can't possibly tell him that we're not getting married right now. I can't ruin his weekend."

"But the longer you let him believe it, the harder it will be to accept." Raven paused and Christie wondered what to say next. She was looking for answers. "Or maybe if you don't tell him, you'll change your mind," Raven added.

"I can't change my mind. I told him what I wanted and needed from a relationship, and he said he understood, but then we... Things heated up, and before long we were both naked and then the alarm rang and he said I'd better get used to it since I was going to be a ranch wife."

"Ugh, that's a problem."

"Exactly! What am I going to do?" Christie said, using a damp finger to blot up cookie crumbs.

"Christie, I don't know. I hardly know Cal. The brothers are like night and day. They barely get along."

"I know they have their differences, and I know Cal was upset about the changes Troy made, but they're both men. And apparently I have a problem understanding men, considering I can't get along with my father, my late husband preferred race cars to me and now Cal believes we're getting married."

Raven paused again. "That could all be coincidence."

Christie felt as if she should pound her head on the table, except that the nice woman at the front counter would probably come running and ask her what was wrong. And then she'd tell her because she was desperate for answers, and the whole county would know. "I really can't decide if I should tell him now and ruin his weekend, or later, and then he'll know I kept something from him."

"Christie, only you can decide what's right. Could you possibly take some time to think about it? Go on to Fort Worth and see how the weekend goes?"

"I guess you're right. I just feel bad putting it off."

"Give him a chance to meet your family, anyway."

"Um, that might be a problem."

"Why?"

"If I bring Cal home, both he and my parents will assume we *are* getting married. The last thing—the very last thing— I want Cal to do is ask for my hand in marriage. There's no telling what my father would say to him."

"What do you mean?"

"My father is an elitist. He refers to Cal as 'that cowboy.' He won't even spend time with Peter because he considers him tainted by the circumstances of his birth."

"Oh. I see what you mean. I'd keep them apart also. You'll find the right thing to say to Cal at the right time."

"Thanks for listening. I'm going to have to talk to him, but

I'll try to find a good time. Maybe after we have some fun with Peter. He's really bonded with the baby."

"That's great. Maybe in the next year or so we'll have a little cousin for Peter."

"Oh, I hope so. Having a baby is just so wonderful."

"Troy has mentioned it, so as soon as we talk about expanding the house, we can discuss children."

"Well, good luck with that. I hope to see you for the wedding, and I'm sure we'll talk before then."

After Christie ended the call, she left a tip and wandered around the antiques store. She'd come to find some accessories for the rooms, and this place seemed full of possibilities. There were a large number of kitschy cowboy- and Western-themed items that appeared to be from the 1950s and 1960s. One booth had lamps, a set of wagon-wheel maple chairs and a large quantity of TV and movie cowboy lunch boxes. They would make a great room with the rather plain maple bedroom set she'd found in Fort Worth. Christie immersed herself in shopping, buying out a large portion of the booth and arranging for delivery.

She went on to find some Hawaiian and tiki items that would work, and found a rare atomic wall clock that was an absolute must for any retro motel. All in all, the day had been a big success. It would be a *great* day if she could figure out what to do about Cal's marriage plans.

ON FRIDAY NIGHT Christie had second thoughts about spending the night in Cal's bed again. Was she leading him on? But after Peter was settled in for the night and the house was quiet, he'd looked at her across the room and she'd come to him, sitting across his lap on the big recliner and making out like teenagers. They went into his bedroom, and she didn't have time to think about where their relationship was going.

She simply enjoyed their time together. Tomorrow would work out.

They left for Fort Worth on Saturday morning, right after morning chores. One of Cal's ranch hands had volunteered to stay at the ranch. The biggest problem was Riley, who couldn't come to the condo. The dog was heartbroken, so Christie had a long talk with him.

"You have to stay here and take care of the house," she told him earnestly. "Do you understand? Stay, Riley. We'll be back on Sunday."

She turned to Cal. He looked at her as if she were crazy. "Make sure you tell Miguel to call us if Riley isn't here. He could run off, you know."

"You're as nutty about dogs as Raven."

"Cal! Do you have any idea how much this dog and Peter have bonded? You could seriously wound their psyches if you separate them."

"You're making this up."

"Prove it."

He shook his head, then grinned, then started to laugh. "Okay, let's go. I'll tell Miguel how sensitive Riley is about our leaving."

"Thank you."

Peter went to sleep on the way to town, and Christie fell silent as she wondered if this was the right time to tell Cal they weren't getting married.

"Are we going to Troy's wedding?" Cal asked before she could decide.

"I'm negotiating with my father on the use of the company jet."

"Fancy. What does he want in return?"

"To make my mother happy. I'm going to talk to her about a benefit for the Kimball she wants me to participate in. I'm not sure what she wants me to do. Hopefully, just donate money. Or maybe put in an appearance. Worst-case scenario, squeeze into a designer gown and strut down a runway."

"You don't like to dress up and strut your stuff?"

"I don't like to be on display."

"You're not a trophy to me, Christie," he said, and she decided right then that she couldn't tell him that they weren't getting married. She smiled at him and drove into Fort Worth, past the turn-off for the stockyards and on to her condo.

ALMOST TWO WEEKS AGO, Christie had asked him if he'd ever considered doing anything but ranching. Cal was even more sure of his answer after spending a day and a half in her condo. The only bright spot had been this morning, when Christie and Peter had given him his first Father's Day card. She'd stamped Peter's handprints in paint or ink. Christie had also given him a sterling silver money clip, engraved with the Rocking C logo. It was a thoughtful gift, which made him feel bad that he hadn't been around last month for her first Mother's Day.

She'd also fixed him a breakfast of waffles, sausage and eggs. The big meal had filled him up, but this afternoon, he'd realized that the pantry, like the rooms, didn't contain much that he liked.

He supposed the furnishings and accessories were attractive, but they weren't his style. He liked really comfortable stuff that you could lounge around on. That you could make love on without worrying about sliding off or messing up the finish. Lots of Christie's furniture was dark, fine-grained leather. It was padded, she'd told Cal, and she'd thought it would be good for Peter when he started to walk.

Cal sat there alone while she was gone with their son to her parents' house and thought about how she'd planned for the future with this leather furniture. How she had never mentioned selling this condo, which must be worth a lot of money due to its downtown location. Didn't condos have monthly maintenance costs? Even after she'd gone to Brody's Crossing and bought the old motel, she'd kept this condo. A place to run back to, or just a weekend place?

Seemed like a really expensive place to have for an occasional trip to town. Most people would stay in a hotel or with their parents, considering they lived just west of town in one of those old, high-priced mansions. Surely there were enough rooms there for one woman and a nine-month-old baby.

Last night both she and Peter had been tense. The baby's stomach had been a little upset, and he was probably teething again. She'd stayed up late with him while Cal had sat around wondering what to do. They hadn't made love, although they'd slept in the same bed. She hadn't mentioned the motel or her plans or their future.

He put his head between his hands and faced reality. Christie hadn't committed to staying in Brody's Crossing forever. He'd *assumed* she would, but she'd never said so. She'd never said she would marry him, either.

He'd wanted to believe it so much, he'd try to make it real.

"I'm an idiot," he said in the silence of the condo. She'd explained that she wanted to make a short visit today to her parents. An obligatory trip. A "happy Father's Day" to a man who had never fully acknowledged his grandson. She said that her father could be rude, and she didn't want to subject Cal to his remarks.

Cal had just spent over a year on the warfront, facing Taliban fighters, drug caravans and hostile villagers. He'd been wounded by shrapnel. He was pretty sure he could handle one rude businessman.

Christie obviously didn't want him in the same room with

her father. She might be not ashamed of him, but she wasn't considering him as a potential husband, either. If she *were* considering marriage, she would have made sure the two of them met, even if the meeting wasn't ideal.

He rose from the couch and paced the wall of windows overlooking the downtown street. Just a couple of blocks away, Sundance Square beckoned, with bars and restaurants. And the bookstore where he and Christie had met. The walls of the condo closed around him. He liked wide-open spaces, his familiar if not stylish house, his functional barn and pastures. He wasn't a man who could be stashed inside a concrete-and-glass condo.

He grabbed his wallet and the key Christie had given him and headed out. Not in the direction of Sundance Square, but someplace else. Somewhere he could be free to think about where he stood in this relationship with Christie and his son.

CHRISTIE DRAGGED HERSELF and her sleepy son into the condo, later than she'd anticipated. She'd gone right after lunch and now it was dinnertime.

"Cal?" There was no answer. Maybe he'd gotten hungry and gone out. But why hadn't he called her cell phone?

She walked into the open living area and placed Peter's carrier, then the diaper bag and her purse on the leather bench. He was getting heavier every day, and the amount of things she needed to carry around hadn't decreased one bit. Before long, she'd need a shopping cart to get out the door. Or perhaps she'd just have to take the stroller everywhere she went.

Sure enough, Cal's key and his wallet were gone, she noticed.

The visit with her parents had been as stressful as she'd anticipated and had taken longer than she'd hoped. Her mother had at least tried to generate some interest in Peter, although her Pekingese, Mr. Boodles, had barked himself into a wheezing attack. Her father hadn't known what to do or say to a baby, and so he'd studied him like a specimen under glass.

"I'm sorry your grandfather is such a sourpuss," she told Peter, making faces at him while she unhooked the straps of the carrier. He finally smiled back, but she could tell he was still tired and cranky.

Peter hadn't taken well to the unsmiling stranger, and had cried whenever he'd looked at his grandfather. Christie had explained that she was extremely busy with the baby and the renovations on the motel, so at least she'd gotten out of anything but a promise to attend the Kimball fundraiser this fall—and sponsor a table. Her father had reminded her that she could deduct the money as a marketing expense if she listed the motel as the sponsor.

To take a deduction, she had to have enough revenue coming in. She sure hoped that was the case. This year's expenses would be a loss, but her accountant had said she could amortize the renovations over several years.

She had the money to take an indefinite loss, but her whole point was to run a successful business. One that could be self-sustaining if necessary. The motel project was truly a labor of love, and she didn't want to give it up on a whim. If she had to leave Brody's Crossing, she'd like to sell the motel and be sure someone else could care for it as she did.

If she had to leave Cal…

She didn't want to leave him. She wanted…what? For him to ask her to stay? To marry him?

Did she want to marry him? She'd told him she would only marry again for love. She wasn't sure if she knew how it felt to be in love. She'd heard no bells, seen no white doves flying, no rainbows in the sky. Cal was steady and quiet and not at all flashy. He'd only brought her flowers one time; they'd barely been on two dates.

But they'd made a baby together. They lived together. They'd made love…again.

Last night she'd missed sleeping in his arms. Being here in Fort Worth, in her condo, had felt awkward, as if Cal were a stranger. When they were together at the ranch, she felt so cherished. She felt as if the rest of the world could go right by and they'd be fine because they had each other. She'd felt safe and happy. She'd felt…loved.

But he'd never told her he loved her. She would only marry someone whom she loved and who loved her. And Cal was the only man she loved.

"I have to talk to your daddy," she told Peter as she lifted him from the carrier. If he didn't offer to say the words, she'd have to ask him directly, whether she felt comfortable doing so or not.

She'd already told him what she wanted from a relationship. Maybe he'd thought that he'd showed her how he felt, just as he'd thought that he'd asked her to marry him when he actually hadn't. Yes, that must be the problem. A simple lack of communication might keep them apart unless she took the first step.

She sure wished Cal had taken the time to get a cell phone. She had no idea how to reach him. And she desperately wanted to go back to the ranch. There, she felt grounded. There, she and Cal could work out any problems and get started on the future.

She heard the lock turn and the door open. She whirled, clutching Peter tightly.

"Thank God you're back," she said. "I'm so ready to go home."

Chapter Thirteen

They had to feed Peter a snack to hold him over until they got back to the ranch. Unfortunately, goldfish crackers and cheese slices didn't satisfy him all the way to Brody's Crossing. In the car, he fussed, threw his toys and was generally crabby. They had to stop and change him, then give him a sippy cup of apple juice. Cal felt even more frustrated because he wanted to talk to Christie. On the other hand, the baby allowed him to put off this conversation.

"Maybe he'll go to sleep early tonight," Cal said as Christie pulled the SRX into the drive and stopped near the back of the house.

"I like to keep him on a schedule," Christie said.

"I know, I just—"

"I'm sorry. I didn't mean to snap. I'm just drained. My parents wore me out. Peter is more fussy than usual. And I want to talk to you, but I know I can't right now." She rested her arms on the steering wheel for a moment, then sat upright.

"I feel the same way, only I didn't spend the afternoon with parents." Cal unbuckled his seat belt and opened the passenger door.

"Where did you go?" she asked, getting out of the car.

"I went for a walk. I ended up at the Water Gardens. It's kind of nice there. More open. The water is peaceful."

"I thought you'd gotten tired of waiting and went out for something to eat," Christie said as she unbuckled Peter.

"No, I just needed to get out."

"I'm sorry we were gone so long."

"It's not that," Cal said, unloading her overnight bag and the diaper bag. "I'm just not a condo kind of guy, Christie. I felt closed in." He unlocked the back door and Riley came bounding out, yipping and running in circles. Yeah, he felt a lot like Riley. Really happy to be out, and back where he belonged.

"Do you remember when you asked if I could see myself doing anything else but ranching?" When she nodded, he continued, "Well, I said then that I couldn't and I mean it even more now. This is who I am."

"I know that, Cal. Why are you saying it again, as if you didn't think I took you seriously?" she asked as she carried Peter into the house.

"Because I thought about us a lot today while you were gone."

As soon as they got into the kitchen, Peter started crying. He reared back in Christie's arms and cut off all conversation. "I can't talk about this right now," she said, holding tight to the squirming baby.

"I know. I didn't mean we should." He went back out, got his overnight bag and the plastic bag of trash and came back into the kitchen. "Would you like me to take Peter so you can fix his dinner?"

"Yes, thank you," she said, handing the baby over.

"Come on, Peter. Let's go outside and see the animals." He held open the back door and the dog ran ahead. He and the baby followed. Slowly, Peter focused on the chickens and the big, loud grackles that had flown into the limbs of the cotton-wood tree. He walked along the fencerow and looked at the dairy cows grazing in the near pasture. The black-and-white animals were beginning to appear "normal" in his pasture, which was rather surprising. He didn't like dairy cows, but he didn't resent them as much as he had a few weeks ago.

Peter calmed down as he focused on the animals. Cal wished he could do the same. How was he going to tell Christie that she'd been right all along, that they shouldn't be together? That he'd been wrong to believe they should get married? That maybe they weren't right for each other just because they had great sex and had made a baby?

Cal took a deep breath. Hell, she'd probably be relieved. She'd said she'd only get married if she loved someone, and she obviously didn't love *him*. He'd forgotten, for a short while, why he was unworthy of her love even if she did agree to marry him. Exhaling deeply, he turned and walked back to the house.

BY THE TIME CHRISTIE got Peter fed, bathed and in his crib, she was exhausted. The day had been exceptionally stressful and it wasn't over yet. Cal had been in a strange mood ever since they'd left Fort Worth, but she had to tell him what she'd realized today. She walked out of the bedroom and left the door open a crack. Looking back once, she smiled at Riley, curled up on the braided rug, projecting happy doggy vibes now that his family was back home.

"I'm glad to be home, too," she whispered to Riley.

She walked down the hall. The television in the living room was silent. In the kitchen, Cal had loaded the dishwasher and locked the back door. Where was he? She walked back down the hall and knocked lightly on his bedroom door.

"Come in," he said.

He was snapping a plaid shirt, which hung loose over his jeans. He wore boots and smelled fresh, as if he'd showered after evening chores.

"I thought I might go out to Dewey's for a while," he said. "I don't imagine too many people that I know will be there on Father's Day, but I'm going anyway."

"Oh," she said, frowning. "What's wrong?"

He paused after the last snap, his expression bleak. Yes, something was definitely wrong. "This weekend made me realize how different we are—about everything. How we live, what we want, how we think about things."

"What do you mean? Are you angry because I went to my parents' house without you? I only did that because of my father."

"Yeah, I heard you, Christie, but I'm a grown man. I've run this ranch since I was twenty years old, I've served active duty in a war zone, and I manage to get along with most folks around here. I think I could have handled meeting your father if you'd wanted me to. The fact is, you didn't want me around him."

"I… It wasn't because of you."

"I think it was. I'm not sure exactly why, but I'm pretty sure you want to keep me as far away from your parents as possible. That reflects on me. You know it does."

Cal was not being fair. "I was trying to protect you from my father's rudeness."

"I'm not a child, Christie. I don't need your protection. I wanted your support, but I don't think you wanted to give me that, either."

"That's so unfair! I'm very supportive of your being a rancher. Or whatever you want to do."

"As long as I go along with my brother's plans, right?"

"I didn't want you to do anything that would violate those contracts he set up. Besides, the ranch is wonderful as it is. I enjoy seeing the different types of animals grazing in the pastures. It's so unusual, and besides, raising bison seems kind of noble. I read about how they were nearly extinct by 1900.

Now there's hundreds of thousands of them. Peter loves seeing them and the chickens, cows and horses when we go for walks outside."

"He's too young to know what he likes, and again, I'm not a child. I don't need you or Troy or Raven—yes, I know that they asked people to watch out for me—standing over me, guiding me as if I'm feeble-minded. I know I'm stubborn and opinionated, and I sometimes say things that I should keep to myself, but dammit, I'm a man. I'm not some lapdog that you can pat on the head occasionally."

"Cal, please don't—"

"Don't what, Christie? Tell the truth? That's exactly what we need to do. And the truth is that we were never going to work out our differences. I tried to railroad you into marrying me at first, and for that, I'm sorry. The truth I learned is that you have certain things you want from a relationship that I'll never be able to give you."

She felt tears roll down her cheeks as she stood in front of him. "Because you don't love me and you never will."

"No, because…because you have no idea what kind of person I really am. You don't know me, and maybe that's the way I wanted it. I could be happy with your decision to stay here and not ask too much of me. I wouldn't have questioned what you needed. But you wanted it all, and babe, I don't have enough inside me to give to anyone."

"How can you say that? You've been wonderful with Peter. You are kind-hearted. I've seen it in the way you relate to other people around here. You're even kind to the dog you didn't want."

He snorted and turned away. "Yeah, I'm so great my mother ran off before my high school graduation. I'm such a wonderful person that I caused the death of my own father."

"You…what?"

He whirled around. "I killed him, that's what. My arrogance. My youth. My brash idea that I knew more than him."

She reached out to put a hand on his arm, but he pulled away. "No, Cal."

"Yes, Christie. If I hadn't challenged my father on his ways, the fact that he thought he always knew the answer, then he'd probably still be alive today. Hell, he'd only be sixty-eight years old right now. He was a soldier, a rancher and a hell of a tough guy. He…he could have been a grandfather."

Cal hung his head and shook it slowly. "He survived the jungles of Vietnam, the trip wires, the snipers, the wet-behind-the-ears first lieutenants. He came back and married, built a new house, had a family. He raised me to inherit this, to continue the tradition and run this ranch he loved. And then I just had to pop off my big mouth, my stupid big mouth, and try to tell him what to do."

"Teenagers always challenge their parents and authority figures in general."

"I was twenty years old, almost twenty-one. I wasn't a kid."

"You said it was an accident. You can't blame yourself."

He stepped back, toward the door. "It was an accident that didn't have to happen. I caused it as much as if I'd broken the lift myself."

"What did you say that was so terrible, Cal? What could you have possibly said that we don't all think at one time or another?"

"I told him that his ideas on running the ranch were all wrong. They were too old, too obsolete. I told him that life on the ranch was boring, and I could see why Troy wanted to leave the next year for college."

Christie felt tears fill her eyes again as she watched the anguish on Cal's face.

"I told him that I'd looked at the bank statements and seen the letter about the loan that was coming due. He was always secretive about the finances, so I knew that would push all his buttons, and I did it anyway."

He looked up at the ceiling, then put his hands on his hips, as if bracing himself. "The round bales of hay he was moving might have crushed his chest, done so much internal damage that it couldn't be repaired, but it was my fault he was in that state of mind."

Christie wiped her eyes and wrapped her arms around herself. Cal looked so lost. He'd obviously beaten himself up over this for years. Would he ever overcome his guilt, or would it haunt him forever? With so much regret inside him, was there room for her and Peter?

Sometimes, she knew, people never got over their pasts. They couldn't get beyond what had happened, what they blamed themselves for.

"So, you see, I did kill my father. I was cocky and immature and ignorant. I didn't know half of what I thought I knew. I pushed him into a rage, then stormed off when he continued to work, continued to ignore my demands."

"It would have been so much better if he'd stopped and talked to you."

"Why would he talk to a cocky kid who'd challenged his way of life? He knew what was best and couldn't imagine that his eldest son, the one he'd groomed to take over the ranch, didn't understand. The last thing he said to me before I stormed off was that I didn't deserve to run this ranch if I didn't believe in it. He said it was a privilege that had to be earned, not a birthright that could be inherited."

"Does Troy know?"

"No! I never told him and he doesn't need to know. What happened was between me and my father."

"Still, couldn't he support you? Wouldn't you feel better if you told him about this?"

He looked at her as if she were speaking in tongues. "You think I want to feel better? No! This is my cross to bear. These are my memories, my reminders of what I did. I can't ever forget."

"So you're going to spend the rest of your life beating yourself up over an accident that happened when you were barely out of your teens?"

"It's part of who I am."

"It's not all of who you are."

"You don't understand."

"You're right, I don't. I accept that it's an important part of your life, but so were the twenty years you spent with your father before the accident. So were the eighteen years you spent with your mother before her mental condition made her leave the family."

Christie took in a deep breath. "We're living in the here and now, not in the past. You have a future with me and Peter, if you want it. Do you, Cal, or do you want to continue to think you're guilty of harming your father?"

"I did harm my father! He'd dead, Christie, because of me."

"He's dead because he had a bad temper, he overreacted, he was secretive about the finances when he probably should have told you the whole situation about the ranch. He's gone because of an accident, not a deliberate act by you."

Cal shook his head.

"I understand more than you think. My father is convinced he's right about everything. He manipulates every situation."

"He's alive, Christie. That's something I can never say about mine." Cal grabbed his wallet off the dresser and picked up his truck keys. "I'm going out for a while. Like I said, I need a little time to think."

"Don't push me away, Cal. Please, let's work through this."

"I can't, Christie." He closed his eyes, then opened them

and said in a softer voice, "I don't know how." Then he turned and walked out the door.

Christie sank to the bed. He'd left her rather than resolve their problems. He'd rather wallow in his grief than move forward. He'd rather be at the bar than with her.

Just like her late husband. Oh, they hadn't fought. Looking back, she supposed he either didn't know how, or simply didn't care enough to make an argument. He simply wanted to pursue his own life, the same one he'd had before they'd married.

She pushed herself up from the mattress and walked down the hall to her bedroom. After checking on Peter, she curled up on her mattress and closed her eyes. Cal was gone for the night, or at least for a while, and she'd never had a chance to tell him she loved him.

Should she even take that chance?

AT FIRST Cal couldn't believe he'd told Christie about causing his father's death. He sure hadn't planned on revealing *that* secret. Then, as he drove to Dewey's, he'd thought perhaps letting it out would make him feel better. Eventually. He didn't expect some big epiphany with trumpets and rays of light. Just something quiet.

He didn't feel any better, even now, sipping his second beer, knowing that someone else on the planet shared the truth of his situation. The fact that the person he'd told was the one he should have been trying most to impress was nagging at him.

You should have told your brother, a little voice inside his head whispered.

"No, not him," he whispered as he held the longneck to his lips.

"Whadja say?" an older cowboy on the bar stool next to him asked. Cal had watched him belt back several shots of

Jack Daniel's, straight up. Was he an alcoholic, or was this a special day? Father's Day. Did the old cowboy have family? It wasn't any of Cal's business.

"Nothing." He really didn't want to start a conversation. He'd come to think, to get away from talking about his troubles.

"Women problems?"

"Yes. No. Not really. Just…life troubles." His life didn't suck, but sometimes it seemed as if happiness lay just out of his reach. For much of the time Christie had been at the ranch, he'd tasted joy. When he thought they were going to get married, he'd latched on tightly to those feelings. But that had been just an illusion, a figment of his imagination. She hadn't agreed, and he'd seen only what he wanted to see.

"Sometimes, your mind plays tricks on you," he said softly.

"That's the truth of it," the old cowboy said. "Why, a few more of these, and sometimes I see the damnedest things," he said with a raspy chuckle.

Cal nodded. Drinking at a bar wasn't the answer. He knew that, but it was something to do, a place to get away from the conversation with Christie that he shouldn't have started in the first place.

Tell your brother, the little voice whispered.

"No," Cal said out loud. "I've got to go." When the voices started talking to you, you were in worse shape than you thought.

"Drive safe," the cowboy said.

"Yeah, I will." Back to the ranch. Back to the reality he'd created.

Back to the woman he'd just started to…what? Love? He wasn't sure he knew how to love.

You love your son, the little voice reminded him.

Yes, he did love Peter. As he'd never loved another person. A pure kind of joyful love that filled him, even when Peter was fussy, especially when he was hurting. The love of a father for his son.

He put a ten on the bar, then looked at the old cowboy again. "Do you have children?" Cal asked.

"Used to," the man said, taking another sip. "I don't know where he is now. We…lost touch when I left his momma."

"I hope you can find him again," Cal said. He didn't add "happy Father's Day" because that would be cruel. Father's Day couldn't be happy if you'd lost track of your son.

Cal walked out into the warm night. He wouldn't lose Peter or let him down. He couldn't disappoint that little boy. He was going to be a good father, a kind man, to his son. He would teach him, but he would also show him love.

Not like your own father, the voice said as he opened the truck door and slid onto the bench seat.

He'd rarely thought about whether his father had loved him. His mother had said she did, but then she'd left. His father had never said the words, but he had said he was proud of him a time or two. He'd shown him how to ranch and care for the heritage. Wasn't that a form of love?

"I'm going to say the words to Peter," he vowed as he drove back to the Rocking C. That wouldn't make him less of a man. He'd be a better father if he could say those words out loud to his son. He should practice here in the truck, while he was alone.

But they didn't come out naturally. For some reason it was really difficult to get the words past his tight lips and frozen jaw.

Damn. He couldn't talk to Christie without dumping out his whole confession, and now he couldn't seem to say the words he needed to tell Peter. What was wrong with him? Was he really too much like his own father?

People had said that he was a chip off the old block, while Troy had looked and acted a little more like their mother, only without the moodiness that had affected her now and then. Their father had been rock-steady. His mood had never varied. His expression had never changed. He was just…Calvin. Veteran, rancher and father. He had known what his life was going to be because that's what his father had taught him.

Christie had asked him once what would happen if Peter didn't want to be a rancher. What if he wanted to be a doctor or some other profession? Cal had dismissed the idea then, but he thought about it now, in the silence of the truck cab as he drove through the darkness. Would he love his son any less because he wasn't a rancher? Was the ranch really more important than family or love?

The idea was hard to accept, but he had to answer—no, it wasn't. The most important thing in Cal's life now was his son, not the Rocking C. He wanted the Rocking C, but he needed Peter.

And Christie.

God, this was confusing. He didn't have any experience in dealing with these personal issues. He'd spent his life as his father had taught him, taking care of the ranch, maintaining that heritage to pass along to his son. Now he had a son, and what was he passing along? Rules and procedures. Knowledge that was, in some cases, out of date. He admitted it now. There were better ways to do things, better resources to take care of the Earth.

Maybe he should think about what his great-great-grandfather had wanted for his family. That had to be different from what Cal's father had taught him. When the first Crawfords had moved here in a wagon, with a small herd of cows and a couple of horses, what had his dreams been?

Cal thought about that as he pulled to a stop near Christie's SRX, which glowed pearly and golden in the mercury vapor lights. She was a far cry from the weathered pioneer woman who'd raised three sons and two daughters on this undeveloped piece of land beginning in the late 1880s. Yet Christie had an inner strength that Cal suspected the ranch wives had shared, or they wouldn't have made it here. Most of them had spent their lives without the companionship of other females, with only their children and husbands to see daily. All of them had worked hard, and he suspected few of them had been truly happy.

Christie had said that having Peter had made her happy. She'd said she needed to create more, like her work renovating the old motel. Cal knew he'd put that project down more than once. He'd been damned negative about spending money on the old building. In her own way, though, she was honoring the past. Not her past, but something of value in the eyes of others, nonetheless. Who was he to say that wasn't valuable?

He'd been an ass, that was for sure. And he'd told her he couldn't give her what she needed, but was that true? Or did it just seem that way because he'd never felt like this before?

He admired Christie, but did he dare to love her as she deserved to be loved? Tomorrow, he was going to do his best to discover if he was capable of love. And he was going to start by telling Peter the words that all children deserved to hear, often and with sincerity. *I love you.* He would say those words out loud, and he'd mean them.

But could he say them to Christie, as well?

Chapter Fourteen

Christie had had a rough night. Her sleep had been interrupted with the sounds her son made while sleeping, the noise of Cal coming back home long before she'd thought he would arrive and the silence of the house as she'd lain curled in bed alone. She'd told herself she couldn't go talk to Cal then, when he was probably wearing boxers or nothing at all.

She needed some time without the distraction of sex. Time to let what he'd said really sink in. He'd given her no clue to his secret before now, except his strong intention to keep to family traditions on the ranch and in his personal life. Looking back, she should have thought about why he was so tied to the past. She'd had other things to consider, however—such as his insistence they get married and his awkward initial bonding with Peter. Plus, she'd been working hard on the motel and dealing with her own family more recently.

Of course, all those details and facts and suppositions didn't change her feelings for Cal.

She slipped into her shower before Peter awoke, while Cal was out doing chores. She dressed quickly, got a cup of coffee from the carafe he'd made earlier, then went back to her room and pulled out her suitcase.

By the time Cal came back into the kitchen, Peter was up

and in his high chair. Christie had made him oatmeal and he wore most of it on his face and bib. He gave Cal a very sloppy grin. Cal smiled back and rubbed his hair. "How are you this morning, Petey?"

"Petey?" Christie asked.

Cal shrugged. "He's a baby. Peter seems so formal."

She scooped some oatmeal off his chin. "So, I need to tell you something," she began, then paused. Her pulse pounded and she was sure that Peter could tell his mommy was nervous.

"What?"

"I'm going to move back to the motel in Graham for a while," she said, her heart racing. Immediately, she regretted her decision. But no, she had to get away.

"Why?" Cal's voice sounded so neutral, so…careful.

"I need time to think, and if I stay here, I'll be too confused. I'm not trying to take Peter away from you, though."

"What, you're leaving him here?"

"No! I mean, I want him to see you, so I thought I'd continue to bring him over every day and have Darla come as usual. That way, you can spend time with him and I can take care of my business. And we can see each other a little and think about what we want."

"I thought you knew what you wanted. Have you changed your mind?"

"What…what do you mean?"

He stepped closer, but not close enough to touch. "You said that you wanted someone who loved you and someone you could love. Is that still what you want?"

"If I was ever going to marry again. That was the prompt, wasn't it?"

"Yes."

"Then, yes, that's what I would want if I were ever to get married."

"Okay, then."

"What does that mean?"

"It means that I understand and respect your decision. I know it wasn't easy for you."

"Um, no, it wasn't." She felt so confused. Why wasn't Cal arguing with her? Why was he being so darn reasonable? She'd half expected him to kiss her silly, try to change her mind. The other option had involved him getting angry and insisting that she wasn't going anywhere.

Or going down on one knee and telling her that he really did love her and want to be with her forever.

"I didn't respect your wishes when you first came here, Christie. I thought that we should get married for what I know now are the wrong reasons. So I'm going to respect your decision now and do my best to work this out."

"What are you going to work out?"

"I spent a lot of time thinking about things last night. I know that I want to be a different kind of dad than my own father was. I also know that I don't know what the hell I'm doing when it comes to relationships. Maybe we both need some time to get a little smarter about us."

She felt confused and excited and full of questions, but Cal was being so agreeable that she knew she should go along for now. "Okay, then. We agree."

He smiled a little. "That's a start."

She smiled back. "Yes, it is. And we have Peter."

"Yes, we do." He looked down at the baby and placed a hand on Peter's head—the only part not covered in oatmeal.

"I'll leave Peter's diaper bag and some things for Darla to use. I'll get the rest of his clothes later."

"Okay. I don't want to rush you. Hell, I don't want you to go at all, but I understand why."

Christie was about to respond when Darla knocked on the

unlocked back door and popped her head around the corner. "Good morning."

"Hi. I was just leaving…" Christie said, "…er, for the motel."

"How's it going?" Darla asked.

"Good. We're on schedule. I still have to find a refinisher, though."

"Maybe you should check with Leo at the hardware store," the babysitter suggested.

"Yes, that's what I've heard." Christie glanced at Cal and saw his mouth tighten. "But I've asked Toni to do that because he is her brother, so I'll just talk to her."

Cal seemed to relax a little.

Christie leaned down and found a clean spot so she could kiss Peter. "I'll see you later, Peter. Be a good boy for your daddy and Darla."

He cried out in protest at Christie's leaving, so she grabbed her purse and tote bag and hurried to the door before he started crying in earnest. "Cal, would you walk me to the car?"

"Sure." He followed her outside.

"I need to tell you something. I was looking for you last night to tell you when…well, when you told me we couldn't be together. I've thought about what I was going to say, and I realized that how I feel doesn't depend on what you told me last night. I still feel the same way."

"What way is that?"

She took a fortifying breath. "I love you, Cal. I love you for a lot of reasons, and it doesn't matter that you haven't forgiven yourself."

"Then why are you leaving me?"

"Because sometimes it's too hard to stay."

"I don't know what that means."

"Maybe we both need to figure it out."

"Christie, I can't promise that I can forgive myself for

what I did. It happened sixteen years ago, and I've lived with it every day since then."

"For our future, I hope you can. Please, just remember that I love you for who you are now, not who you were sixteen years and one day ago. Everything you've gone through has made you the man you are now."

"I'll try," he promised.

"That's all you can do, and that's why we need some time."

"See you later, Christie," Cal said.

"Yes…later." Later, when she came back for her suitcase and her son and moved them into the motel in Graham.

AT NIGHT, THE HOUSE he'd grown up in and had lived alone in for sixteen years seemed way too quiet. Except for the sound of the television, the only noise came from Riley's loud sighs and tapping toenails as he walked from the living room to the kitchen to Christie and Peter's bedroom.

"At least you get to stay with Peter during the day," Cal told the dog, who sighed again and laid his head on his front legs. Cal had spent time with Peter in the afternoon, after the baby's nap, and had really enjoyed listening to his baby babble, getting pelted with goldfish crackers and having his fingers chewed on by teething gums.

When he wasn't with the baby, though, he'd thought about his life here on the ranch, his past and his future. He realized how comfortable he'd become with the memories, both bad and good. He hadn't been challenged by anyone in years, and then first his brother, then Christie had shaken him out of his comfort zone. Especially the day she'd moved out, when she'd told him that she loved him. He hadn't expected that; he hadn't known how to respond.

Every afternoon, when Darla left for the day and Christie came to pick up Peter, Cal held Peter in his arms, looked him in the eyes and told him that he loved him. The words still threatened to bring a lump to his throat, especially when Peter grinned at him and gave him a baby version of a sloppy kiss.

After four nights alone, he felt the need to talk to Troy. They'd been a little too far apart in age to be totally bonded as brothers when they were growing up. And then Troy had gone away to college and Cal hadn't. As a matter of fact, their father had never even considered college for Cal. He didn't need formal education, Calvin Crawford had said, because as eldest son he was going to run the ranch. Everything he needed to know would be learned right there.

Their mother had started a college fund for Troy, so he'd gone off to earn a business degree. While Cal had been struggling to hold the ranch together, Troy had been hundreds of miles away in Austin. They'd never really been close after that, but maybe they could start over as adults.

Cal dialed his brother's number from the phone in the office. "Hey, little brother," he said after they said hello. "I need some advice."

There was a long pause, then Troy said, "Who are you and what have you done with Cal?"

"Very funny. I'm serious. Christie moved out Monday because I…well, a couple of things I did, and she said we needed some time apart to think things over."

Troy groaned. "Man, I leave you alone for a few weeks, and you've already run her off. What happened?"

"I never thought she was serious about staying. But let me tell you why." He explained to Troy about the condo, the Father's Day visit to Fort Worth, and then fudged a little on the conversation with Christie that night. She'd told him to talk to Troy about what had happened, but he didn't think he could tell his brother why their father had died. All Troy knew was that there had been an accident.

"So, I said some things that maybe I shouldn't have said. I think I was trying to run her off, to tell you the truth. I guess I…I didn't feel worthy of her."

"You're serious?"

"Well, yeah."

Cal sighed. "How hurtful?"

"I told her that I couldn't give her what she needed and wanted."

And then she'd told him that she loved him anyway.

Cal imagined his brother shaking his head. Then Troy said, "You have dug yourself a hole. The only advice I can give you is to tell her the truth about why you said those things. If you were scared of commitment, tell her so. If you were mistaken about your feelings, tell her. Swallow your pride. Don't let it go on too long."

Troy didn't know it, but he could have been talking about Cal's other problem, the secret of their father's death. Should he swallow his pride and tell his brother what had happened? Now? Right before his wedding?

"Hey, are you okay?" Troy asked.

"Yeah, I'm fine. Just thinking."

"Don't think too much. Take action. Women like men who are decisive."

"Being decisive is what got me into this situation."

"Hey, you have to make the *right* decisions," Troy advised. "Does this mean that Christie and the baby aren't coming to the wedding?"

"I don't know, but I'll talk to her tomorrow."

"Hey, ask her out on a date."

"I already tried that."

"Once? Try again."

They ended the call after exchanging more information about the wedding, which was coming up in a little over two weeks. Raven sent her greetings, which was nice, and when Cal ended the call, he felt a lot more like he was part of a family.

CHRISTIE KEPT HERSELF very busy with the Sweet Dreams renovations. The furniture refinisher, who was even more attractive than Leo Casale, was working on all the bedroom sets, chairs and tables from his shop. Good thing Cal hadn't seen Michael, who could put some of those home improvement hunks to shame. Of course, he didn't have the character of an army veteran who'd put his life into the land.

She saw Cal daily and missed him like crazy at night. She missed curling up with him on the couch and sleeping next to him. Even though their time together had been brief, she missed him as though they'd been together for years.

And she was more sure now than ever that she loved unequivocally. She was willing to give him time to work through his personal issues. She was willing to help. Whatever Cal needed was fine with her.

He'd asked her if she wanted to go on a date. She had seriously considered going but, in the end, had decided that they shouldn't. Until he could tell her what she needed to hear, she didn't see the point of going out to dinner. As far as she was concerned, they knew what they needed to know about each other.

She'd also told him that as far as she was concerned, they were all still going to the wedding. The corporate jet would be at their disposal. They'd have to drive to Alliance Airport just north of Fort Worth and fly out of there on the Friday before the wedding.

She also discovered that both she and Cal would be in the Fourth of July parade in Brody's Crossing, one week before the wedding. Not riding together, but both participating. He'd be on the VFW float while she had arranged for a vintage convertible Thunderbird with a magnetic sign on each door advertising the motel. She would ride in the backseat, sitting up high.

She'd even had a new outfit created for herself, with a short-sleeve white blouse and a poodle skirt that would lie in a half circle over the seat. Instead of a felt dog, however, her skirt had the motel's crescent moon and baby logo stitched on it. Her hair was drawn back in a ponytail tied with a bright pink silk scarf.

Peter was going to stay with Darla on Main Street, but he'd be dressed in jeans and a white T-shirt with some cute little black-and-white oxfords she'd found in the baby department of the discount store in Graham. Darla had offered to wear a T-shirt with the Sweet Dreams logo on it, and capri pants.

The parade would be fun and the first step in her marketing plan for the motel. Hopefully, the photographer from the newspaper in Graham would get some great pictures.

If only she felt as optimistic about her personal life. She and Cal seemed stuck in a rut. They were getting along great, but as far as she could tell, they weren't moving forward. Of course, he'd completely bonded with his son. Peter was even giving him kisses, a new skill he'd just learned.

The staging area for the parade was the high school stadium parking lot. The owner of the Thunderbird was already there when Christie drove up. She joined him, chatted for a moment, then looked around for the VFW float.

All the way across the parking lot, veterans in their uniforms milled about the truck that would pull the flatbed trailer decorated in red, white and blue bunting. She saw Cal immediately, standing tall and looking very buff in his green dress uniform. He was turned away from her, though, so she couldn't see his face. She knew him, though.

"Miss Christie?" the owner of the Thunderbird asked.

"Hmm?" She turned away reluctantly. "Yes?"

"We're ready to get in line."

"Of course." He helped her climb into the back, then onto

the rear seat. She spread her skirt across the white tufted vinyl. "This car is beautiful," she said. "If you ever decide to sell it, will you let me know?"

"I sure will."

Within a few minutes, the line of vehicles pulled out toward Main Street, approximately a half mile away. They caught up with the bands and twirlers and little princesses, and everyone got in order. With a patriotic flourish of flags and marching music, the parade got under way. Christie was so excited. Although she'd traveled all over the world and had participated in some of the most elegant events in Washington, D.C., and Austin, she'd never felt closer to the spirit of America than she did then.

Downtown Main Street in Brody's Crossing was only three blocks long, so Christie knew that the parade would turn right on Market Street and go by the farmers' market and butcher shop, then turn right again and travel past the vacant train station. From the crowd on Main Street, however, she guessed this was where most people chose to see the bands, floats and vehicles.

She waved as if she were a princess herself. She'd hired two teenage girls to walk beside the car and pass out discount tickets in the form of gold cardboard Sweet Dreams Motel room keys. The opening wasn't for two months, but Christie had hopes that the ten rooms would fill up fast for the holidays and weekends. The owner's suite was almost ready for occupancy.

Just as they got to the corner of Main and Commerce, the parade slowed. She looked ahead to see if there was a problem, but all she could see was a baton-twirling act. She sat in the hot sun and looked for Peter and Darla. She finally spotted them in the shade beneath the bank building awning. Waving, she threw Peter a kiss and laughed when Darla waved his chubby little arms. A photographer snapped a few photos then, and Christie hoped she could get one for her scrapbook.

The twirlers finished their act, but to Christie's surprise, the parade didn't start up again. Instead, someone stepped out of the crowd, marched to the middle of the intersection, held up a violin and began to play one of her favorite melodies from *Phantom of the Opera*. Before she could figure out whether this person was part of the parade or simply an inspired by-stander, a murmur went through the crowd. She turned in time to see a flash of army green, then two strong arms lifted her from the back of the Thunderbird.

She squealed as he carried her with long strides to the front of the car and placed her on the hood. The metal was hot, so she tucked her skirt around her as Cal stared intently into her eyes. Then, as the crowd quieted and the sun beat down on them, he went to one knee and looked up at her.

"Christie, I'm not the brightest man in the world. Some-times it takes a while for me to realize what a wonderful treasure was dropped into my arms a year and a half ago when I met you in Fort Worth. Sometimes it takes drastic action to make me see the truth that was right under my roof."

He paused and placed his hand in the pocket of his dress uniform, right above the service ribbons and the Purple Heart he'd earned in Afghanistan. Her hands went to her mouth as she realized what was happening, right now in the middle of Main Street. She didn't have much time to think, though, because he took her hand in his and said, "Christie, I love you with all my heart. I know we deserve to be happy, and I think we'll only be happy together. Forever."

His voice wavered a little, and the tears in her eyes blurred his features as she stared at him. "Christine Simmons, will you marry me?"

She started to cry and all she could do was nod and hold

out her hand, the one with the ring finger, where he placed an old-fashioned, white-gold filigree engagement ring with a small diamond.

"This was my grandmother's ring," Cal said softly. "I know you're used to more, but I hope you'll accept this ring because it comes with my love."

"Yes," she finally managed to say, then held out her arms. He rose from the concrete and took her in his arms, pulling her off the Thunderbird. He twirled her as she held on tightly, burrowing against the wool of his uniform.

When they were both dizzy, he stopped, and only then did she notice the cheering crowd, the marching band playing a triumphant song, the friends and neighbors taking photos. Darla walked over with Peter, and they all hugged to more cheers from along Main Street.

"How did you arrange all this?"

"You seem to be a personal friend of the mayor," Cal said.

"I feel as if I should take off your hat and throw it in the air," Christie said, grinning so much that her cheeks hurt.

"Don't do it. I only have one, and I need to finish the parade," Cal answered.

She laughed and took Peter. Cal wrapped his arm around them both as Darla stepped back. "I must say this…" Christie told the crowd, which included all of the people she'd met since moving there last month "…in Brody's Crossing, you really know how to throw a parade."

They cheered again, and Christie reached up, cupped her future husband's jaw and kissed him for all the world to see. When they broke apart, she whispered to him, "I'm going to make a fantastic ranch wife."

"I always knew you would," Cal said, and climbed into the turquoise Thunderbird with her and Peter to finish the parade.

Epilogue

"I'm really happy for you, bro," Cal said to Troy as they sat on the deck of the resort overlooking the bay. The sun was setting in the Gulf, and the ripples in the water reflected orange and pink and purple.

Troy's loose bow tie flapped in the Florida breeze against his partially unbuttoned tuxedo shirt. He took a pull from the longneck while music drifted out the half-opened door to the reception. "Thanks. I'm happy for you, too. When's the ceremony?"

"Probably in October, if everything goes well with the opening of the motel. Christie wants to have it in Brody's Crossing, but her mother is pitching a fit to have a fancy shindig in Fort Worth, and her father is threatening to disown her if she marries a cowboy."

"Sounds like the showdown at the OK Corral."

"Actually, Christie will do whatever she wants. She always does. And her father, we've both learned, has a bark that's worse than his bite. When I met him, I knew right off he was a tough businessman, but he's not so tough when it comes to his wife and daughter. And I think he's starting to get taken in by Peter. I actually saw 'Grampa Simmons,' as Christie says just to annoy him, smile at Peter when no one was looking."

"I wish our parents had lived long enough to see their grandkids. Raven and I are thinking of starting a family real soon. Her biological clock is ticking."

"Yeah, Christie and I want a brother or sister for Peter. I just don't know. That doctor in Europe said she couldn't have children, but she didn't have any trouble getting pregnant with Peter. Since we just got back together, she hasn't been to the doctor yet to see if there's any problems now. I hope not, because she's a great mother."

"What did you guys decide about Peter's name?"

"It's staying the same. I'm not going to burden him with a long tradition of names and expectations. He's going to be able to decide what he wants to do with his life."

"Good for you." Troy took another sip of beer. "Raising kids must be hard."

"It's easier when you have a good woman by your side."

"Yeah, I think Raven will be wonderful. She's about the most nurturing person I've ever met."

They each took a sip of beer and watched the orange sun sink into the Gulf.

"Troy, there's something I need to tell you about our dad's accident, but I don't want to do it now, on your wedding day. I'm going to talk you soon, though."

"What's going on?"

"It's just something I need to get off my chest. Something I've never told you before."

"Tell me now."

Cal shook his head. "No, not today. This is a day of celebrations and new beginnings. What I have to say is from the past. It can wait."

"You've got me wondering."

"I know, but forget about it for now. Have fun with your

new bride, have a great time on your honeymoon and I'll talk to you soon, okay?"

"If you say so," Troy said with a frown. "I do trust you."

"I trust you, too," Cal said, smiling at his little brother. "After all, we're family."

LATER THAT NIGHT, after the reception had wound down and everyone had gone to their rooms, Cal pulled his loose bow tie from around his neck, unbuttoned another stud on the shirt and removed the uncomfortable dress shoes he'd been forced to wear with the tuxedo. He propped his feet on the tropical-print ottoman and leaned his head back against the sofa.

The flight down on the Simmons Hotel Group private jet had been a truly luxurious experience. All Cal's previous flights had been spent in crammed commercial coach seats or military transport planes. Peter had slept through much of the trip, and although the ride had been pretty smooth, Christie had arrived feeling a little queasy.

She'd perked up after a day at the resort, although she'd been in the bathroom for quite a while tonight. He hoped she hadn't eaten any weird vegetarian dish that had upset her stomach. Raven had planned what she called an "eclectic" menu. He was just about to go check on Christie when she shuffled into the living room. Her hair was messy and she was barefoot. She looked a little shell-shocked.

"What's wrong, babe?" he asked as he took her hand. Hers felt a little cold and clammy.

"Do you remember that first night we were back together at the ranch?"

"You mean when you and Peter moved back in?"

"No, I mean when we were living there last month and you and I got back together, so to speak. Physically."

Cal grinned. "Oh, yeah. I remember."

"Remember when Peter woke up in the middle of the night, and I went in and gave him a pacifier?"

"Um, not really. I mean, I guess, but I was sleepy."

"Me, too. I climbed back into bed and we…um, got together again."

Cal raised an eyebrow. "Ah, yeah, now I remember."

She punched him lightly on the arm. "Well, we must have been really sleepy because, now that I think about it, we didn't use any protection."

He frowned. "I don't remember that. Why are you thinking about it now?"

"Because…" she said, looking a little bewildered, "…I'm pregnant."

His eyes shot open, his feet hit the floor and he turned to Christie. "You are? You're sure?"

"I got the most reliable home pregnancy test kit I could buy. You are going to be a father again come next March."

He looked at her for a moment, then broke into a grin so wide his cheeks felt like balloons. "Are you okay with this? Because I'm great. I'm so happy."

She took a deep breath, then smiled. "I'm happy. It's just a little shocking to think I went from believing I'd never have children to getting pregnant every single time we have sex without protection." She swatted his arm again. "Stop being so damned virile."

"Hey, you're the one who's so fertile."

"Am not."

"Are, too." He pulled her into his arms and kissed her. "I'm really, really happy."

"I know. I'm happy, too. But now you have to marry me," she said, holding up her ring finger where his grandmother's ring glistened in the soft light. "Because I'm not going to keep having babies with you if you don't make me an honest woman."

"I'll marry you tomorrow if we can find a way. Hey, we could hijack Daddy's plane to Las Vegas!"

"Hmm," Christie said, twining her fingers with his, "that's something to think about. But, no, I want to get married in Brody's Crossing, with all our friends and neighbors in attendance." She paused, then said, "You know, at one time I told myself that I could do anything I wanted, and I thought that meant I needed to go from one career or one interest to another. Whatever I enjoyed, I could do. Now I know that what I really want is to be on the Rocking C with you, Peter, our future child or children and our friends. I can't think of anything I'd enjoy more."

He put his arm around her shoulder and held her close. "We're going to have a great life."

"Yes, we will," she said, yawning behind her hand. "Just you, me and our thirteen children."

"We're going to need a bigger house," he said. "Fortunately, there's a Crawford tradition of building a house for a new bride."

"Good. Let's make it nice and big, just in case we have future 'happy accidents.'"

Cal laughed and hugged her close. Soon her breathing slowed and her body relaxed. He continued smiling as he leaned down and kissed her blond hair. "Sweet dreams, my love."

* * * * *

*Come back to Brody's Crossing for Toni Casale's story about her first love's return to town—
and his quest to win her heart.
A TEXAN RETURNS is available in December 2008,
only from Harlequin American Romance!*

Love Inspired
HISTORICAL

*Powerful, engaging stories of romance, adventure and faith
set in the past—when life was simpler and faith played
a major role in everyday lives.*

*See below for a sneak preview of
HIGH COUNTRY BRIDE
by Jillian Hart*

*Love Inspired Historical—love and faith
throughout the ages*

Silence remained between them, and she felt the rake of his gaze, taking her in from the top of her wind-blown hair where escaped tendrils snapped in the wind to the toe of her scuffed, patched shoes. She watched him fist up his big, work-roughened hands and expected the worst.

"You never told me, Miz Nelson. Where are you going to go?" His tone was flat, his jaw tensed as if he were still fighting his temper. His blue gaze shot past her to watch the children going about their picking up.

"I don't know." Her throat went dry. Her tongue felt thick as she answered. "When I find employment, I could wire a payment to you. Rent. Y-you aren't think-ing of bringing the sher-rif in?"

"You think I want *payment?*" He boomed like winter thunder. *"You think I want rent money?"*

"Frankly, I don't know what you want."

"I'll tell you what I don't want. I don't want—" His words cannoned in the silence as he paused, and a passing pair of geese overhead honked in flat-noted tones. He grimaced, and it was impossible to know what he would say or do.

She trembled, not from fear of him, she truly didn't believe he would strike her, but from the unknown. Of being forced to take the frightening step off the only safe spot she'd known since she'd lost Pa's house.

When you were homeless, everything seemed so fragile, so easily off balance, for it was a big, unkind world for a woman alone with her children. She had no one to protect her. No one to care. The truth was, she'd never had those things in her husband. How could she expect them from any stranger? Especially this man she hardly knew, who was harsh and cold and hardhearted.

And, worse, what if he brought in the law?

"You can't keep living out of a wagon," he said, still angry, the cords still straining in his neck. "Animals have enough sense to keep their young cared for and safe."

Yes, it was as she'd thought. He intended to be as cruel about this as he could be. She spun on her heel, pulling up all her defenses, and was determined to let his upcoming hurtful words roll off her like rainwater on an oiled tarp. She grabbed the towel the children had neatly folded and tossed it into the laundry box in the back of the wagon.

"Miz Nelson. I'm talking to you."

"Yes, I know. If you expect me to stand there while you tongue lash me, you're mistaken. I have packing to get to." Her fingers were clumsy as she hefted the bucket of water she'd brought for washing—she wouldn't need that now—and heaved.

His hand clasped on the handle beside hers, and she could feel the life and power of him vibrate along the thin metal. "Give it to me."

Her fingers let go. She felt stunned as he walked away, easily carrying the bucket that had been so heavy to her, and quietly, methodically, put out the small cooking fire. He did not seem as ominous or as intimidating—somehow—as he stood in the shadows, bent to his task, although she couldn't say why that was. Perhaps it was because he wasn't acting the way she was used to men acting. She was quite used to doing all the work.

Jamie scurried over, juggling his wooden horses, to watch. Daisy hung back, eyes wide and still, taking in the mysterious goings-on.

He is different when he's near to them, she realized. He didn't seem harsh, and there was no hint of anger—or, come to think of it, any other emotion—as he shook out the empty bucket, nodded once to the children and then retraced his path to her.

"Let me guess." He dropped the bucket onto the tailgate, and his anger appeared to be back. Cords strained in his neck and jaw as he growled at her. "If you leave here, you don't know where you're going and you have no money to get there with?"

She nodded. "Yes, sir."

"Then get you and your kids into the wagon. I'll hitch up your horses for you." His eyes were cold and yet they were not unfeeling as he fastened his gaze on hers. "I have an empty shanty out back of my house that no one's living in. You can stay there for the night."

"What?" She stumbled back, and the solid wood of the tailgate bit into the small of her back. "But—"

"There will be no argument," he bit out, interrupting her. "None at all. I buried a wife and son years ago, what was most precious to me, and to see you and them neglected like this—with no one to care—" His jaw ground again and his eyes were no longer cold.

Joanna didn't think she'd ever seen anything sadder than Aiden McKaslin as the sun went down on him.

* * * * *

Don't miss this deeply moving story,
HIGH COUNTRY BRIDE,
available July 2008
from the new Love Inspired Historical line.

Also look for SEASIDE CINDERELLA
by Anna Schmidt,
where a poor servant girl and a wealthy merchant prince
might somehow make a life together.

REQUEST YOUR FREE BOOKS!
2 FREE NOVELS PLUS 2
FREE GIFTS!

Heart, Home & Happiness!

YES! Please send me 2 FREE Harlequin American Romance® novels and my 2 FREE gifts (gifts are worth about $10). After receiving them, if I don't wish to receive any more books, I can return the shipping statement marked "cancel." If I don't cancel, I will receive 4 brand-new novels every month and be billed just $4.24 per book in the U.S. or $4.99 per book in Canada, plus 25¢ shipping and handling per book and applicable taxes, if any*. That's a savings of close to 15% off the cover price! I understand that accepting the 2 free books and gifts places me under no obligation to buy anything. I can always return a shipment and cancel at any time. Even if I never buy another book from Harlequin, the two free books and gifts are mine to keep forever.

154 HDN EEZK 354 HDN EEZV

Name _____ (PLEASE PRINT)

Address _____ Apt. #

City _____ State/Prov. _____ Zip/Postal Code _____

Signature (if under 18, a parent or guardian must sign)

Mail to the **Harlequin Reader Service:**
IN U.S.A.: P.O. Box 1867, Buffalo, NY 14240-1867
IN CANADA: P.O. Box 609, Fort Erie, Ontario L2A 5X3

Not valid to current subscribers of Harlequin American Romance books.

Want to try two free books from another line?
Call 1-800-873-8635 or visit www.morefreebooks.com.

* Terms and prices subject to change without notice. N.Y. residents add applicable sales tax. Canadian residents will be charged applicable provincial taxes and GST. Offer not valid in Quebec. This offer is limited to one order per household. All orders subject to approval. Credit or debit balances in a customer's account(s) may be offset by any other outstanding balance owed by or to the customer. Please allow 4 to 6 weeks for delivery. Offer available while quantities last.

Your Privacy: Harlequin is committed to protecting your privacy. Our Privacy Policy is available online at www.eHarlequin.com or upon request from the Reader Service. From time to time we make our lists of customers available to reputable third parties who may have a product or service of interest to you. If you would prefer we not share your name and address, please check here. ☐

HAR08R

SPECIAL EDITION™

NEW YORK TIMES BESTSELLING AUTHOR

DIANA PALMER

A brand-new Long, Tall Texans novel

HEART OF STONE

Feeling unwanted and unloved, Keely returns
to Jacobsville and to Boone Sinclair, a rancher
troubled by his own past. Boone has always
seemed reserved, but now Keely discovers a
sensuality with him that quickly turns to love. Can
they each see past their own scars to let love in?

*Available September 2008
wherever you buy books.*

Lawyer Audrey Lincoln has sworn off
love, throwing herself into her work
instead. When she meets a much younger
cop named Ryan Mercedes, all her logic
is tossed out the window, and Ryan is
determined that he will not let the issue
of age come between them. It is not until
a tragic case involving an innocent child
threatens to tear them apart that Ryan
and Audrey must fight for a way to
finally be together....

Look for

TRUSTING RYAN

by Tara Taylor Quinn

Available July
wherever you buy books.

Harlequin American Romance is
celebrating its 25th anniversary
just in time to make your
Fourth of July celebrations
sensational with Kraft!

BEST 30-MINUTE BARBECUED RIBS

Prep time: Total: Makes:
20 minutes   30 minutes   6 servings,
                                     about 4 ribs each

4 lb pork baby back ribs
1 cup BULL'S-EYE Original Barbecue Sauce or
  KRAFT Original Barbecue Sauce

CUT ribs into 2-rib sections.

PLACE ribs in Dutch oven or large saucepan. Add enough cold
water to cover ribs completely; cover with lid. Bring to boil. Reduce
heat to medium-low; cover. Simmer 20 minutes; drain.

(Continued on next page)

BEST 30-MINUTE BARBECUED RIBS
(continued)

PREHEAT grill to medium heat. Grill ribs 10 minutes or until ribs are cooked through, turning occasionally and brushing generously with the barbecue sauce.

Kraft Kitchens' Tips

Serving Suggestion:
Serve with a hot baked potato and a crisp mixed green salad tossed with your favorite KRAFT Dressing.

Use Your Microwave:
Cut ribs into sections as directed. Place in large microwavable bowl. Add 1/2 cup water. Microwave on high 20 minutes, stirring gently after 10 minutes; drain. Grill as directed.

Each Harlequin American Romance book
in June contains a different recipe from
the world's favorite food brand, Kraft.
Collect all four to have a complete
Fourth of July meal right at your fingertips!

For more great meal ideas please visit
www.kraftfoods.com.

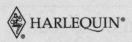

HARLEQUIN®

American ★ Romance®

COMING NEXT MONTH

www.eHarlequin.com

HARCNM0608